Trick and Treats

A WITCHY CANDY SHOP MYSTERY BOOK 1

NYX HALLIWELL

Beach
Path
Publishing

Tricks and Treats, A Witchy Candy Shop Mystery, Book 1

©2024 Nyx Halliwell

ISBN: 978-1-964028-01-9

Chapter One

Horns blare, echoing off the domed ceiling high above my head. A dozen pixies appear out of thin air, forming a circle that hovers over the throne room dais. A bubble forms inside their boundary, and a layer of it peels away, allowing the royal couple to step through the portal.

The queen wears her finest gown of green with threads of gold shot through it, her platinum hair swept high on her head. Not a strand is out of place, with tiny gold and blue butterflies flitting about the top, forming her crown.

With reserved deference, the king escorts her to a crystal throne. He is also in full regale, including his favorite brocade jacket of the finest red velvet. His chest displays rows of medals that twinkle in the sunlight streaming through the generous tall windows of the room.

Gathered nobles quiet at their appearance, but a low buzz of anticipation hums around me, raising the hair on my arms. The Council of Advisers gathers in the arena to my right while the Queen's entourage of ladies-in-waiting sinks into their seats to my left. Behind their generous lashes and under their arched brows, they sneak peeks at me. Shock over my actions is evident on their faces and in the words they whisper behind their gloved hands. A few run bold gazes over my disheveled appearance and wrinkle their noses.

I lift my chin in defiance, ignoring the odor of charred satin and burnt hair engulfing me.

Alden Sternbridge, the High Inquisitor, rises from his seat among the advisers. Dressed in a midnight blue tailcoat that skims the floor, his lean body appears even thinner than it is.

Under most circumstances, his very presence shushes the crowd, but today, they refuse to be contained. The royal family's daughter is on trial, and their excitement leaps from person to person, fueling curiosity and no small amount of perverted glee.

"How the precious candy witch has fallen," one snickers loud enough for me to hear.

Indeed, I have, and the consequences, as I feel my mother's flinty gaze land on me, are unthinkable. To have let her down and tarnished my reputation beyond repair is to have broken my oath to the kingdom of Ever After. Never in my wildest dreams could I have imagined such an indiscretion of this magnitude.

If only I could remember exactly what happened.

Izzy's dead. My stomach lurches, and I clamp my teeth to keep from losing the contents of my stomach.

To distract my spiraling thoughts from the hole in my heart, I catch the eye of the scornful woman. "You'll miss my cherry bonbons," I mutter. She is a regular at my shop—the one that no longer exists. "And my fruity toadstools."

Her gaze flicks away, my words sinking home. My miniature mushroom-shaped confections are renowned for their pretty caps in all colors and flavors. I always carry a few for when my energy wanes. Even one gives a boost and will banish melancholy or worry.

Two are currently in a hidden pocket of my skirt, and I wish my shackled hands could reach them. I could certainly use their sweetness to uplift me at this horrible moment.

It's been more than a hundred years since the citizenry of our land has gathered in the throne room for a disciplinary hearing. Never has one been held for someone of my standing.

Never.

Sternbridge clears his throat loud enough for it to bounce off the walls. This does little to silence the gossipers. Their voices continue to rise and fall, although muted, and even the tinkle of laughter reaches my ears.

A reluctant hush rolls over the room when the Queen casts her quelling stare onto them. Her sharp silver eyes contain the power of a natural-born leader, and while she has been a kind and generous matriarch, she holds the life of each individual here in the palm of her hand.

The King—the father who taught me how to skim rocks and read the Old Tongue— will not look at me, his fingers toying with the cuffs of his jacket. Taking his own throne, he is resplendent, the sun caressing his golden hair and deep blue eyes. Features I've inherited.

The Queen flicks her attention to him for a split second, causing his fingers to stop their movement. Then she nods at the High Inquisitor to proceed.

Once more, Sternbridge clears his throat, the sound like

sandpaper in my ears. "We gather here today to enact justice for the crime of murder against the faery princess of the Black Heart Court, Isadora Ravenswood."

A lump forms in my throat. *Murder.* I have killed a royal. Worse, I have taken the life of my best friend.

How? Why? It's unthinkable. I would never do such a thing.

Would I?

Izzy would no doubt smirk at being labeled "fair." Her mahogany hair is—*was*—the envy of everyone, her obsidian eyes always full of mischief. While she was the crown princess of her court, a place of black hearts, lies, and deception, she was not like her family. Not like the mother who bore her, nor the generations of dark witches and other treacherous beings intent on destroying the peace that has reigned here for a century.

Beyond the walls of the throne room, the roar of the gathering crowd—primarily those from the various courts—rises in a crescendo, angry citizens making their presence known. They will demand blood—mine—as recompense.

"The proof?" the King asks with no amount of weakness in his voice, even as his attention finally lands on me. As the High Fae ruler over all the courts, he must be strong for the kingdom, but I see the profound disappointment at what he must do. "Present it to us."

I'll be given no legal counsel nor a trial like humans extol. Manipulating the truth is impossible in our faery tale world, denying guilt equally so. My friend's blood is on my hands—literally—and her magic essence coats my body, leaving streaks of sooty residue on my skin.

At his command, the portal fairies flutter about,

expanding the space between them. The opaque bubble becomes a screen. I hold my breath as Izzy appears, waiting for the scene to play out.

The double doors behind me burst open. The force is so great that they bang against the stone walls, nearly shattering in the wakeful anger of Veramis Ravenswood, Queen of the Black Heart Court.

The crowd gasps.

Marching up the gilded carpet, she ignores them, a ball of flickering fire crackling in the palm of her hand. There can be no doubt who it is meant for.

Fair enough. An eye for an eye, as the humans say. I shut both of mine as her cry of vehement grief erupts from crimson lips. It screeches over the walls and splinters the glass panes of the windows.

No burning flame touches me, however. Rather, an icy shield springs up, wrapping me in frosty air and sucking the oxygen from my lungs. Another unified gasp erupts at both Veramis' audacity to mete out her personal retaliation and Queen Lethia's defiance of it with her air magic.

I blink and witness the ugly threat that crosses Veramis' face as she points a black, glossy nail at those who sit on the highest thrones of the land. "You would deny me vengeance? Of course, you would show favor to her! All the years and the endless claims that you care about *all* of us, including *my* court, and yet you allow her to live?"

The King rises to his feet slowly, deliberately. All in the room rear back from the absolute anger radiating off him. "The truth will speak for itself, and she will be sentenced accordingly. Your retaliation, while understandable, is not acceptable nor necessary."

Every mouth in the place drops, including mine. Even Queen Lethia seems stunned into silence. Veramis recoils as if he has slapped her.

He speaks in accordance with the rules. While acts such as mine are exceptionally rare, no one in Ever After is allowed to repay violence. Only the High Fae Court doles out discipline.

Sentenced accordingly. His words ring in my ears. That there is any question as to my guilt, or potential options regarding my punishment, is shocking.

It also gives me hope.

Does he believe me that I have no memory of the event?

He is an optimist. Yet, the guilt I feel over what has happened eats at my heart like the flames of Veramis' fireball. My precious Izzy is gone, and I'm to blame.

"I'm so sorry," I utter, the words like razor blades on my tongue. "She was my best friend."

The Shadow Queen strikes me, cutting through the magical ice shield with such force I tumble backward. As the crowd jumps to its feet with outrage, my own feet tangle in the folds of my ruined sky-blue skirt. I topple to the hard marble floor.

The chaos drowns out the clank of my metal shackles. The guards do not help me up, as they would have only hours ago, yet they do intervene before Izzy's mother can strike me again.

"Veramis Ravenswood." Magic amplifies my mother's voice. All those around me fall quiet at the command in her tone. "As the King said, you are rightfully upset, and your desire for vengeance is to be expected. The seriousness of the crime will be taken into account, as will your wishes. To participate in these proceedings, take a seat"—she indicates the section reserved for the council—"and remain silent unless I command you to speak. If you do not, you will be removed."

Veramis snarls. Her cutting beauty is vicious, giving her the appearance of the evil witch of faery tale fame. "I will stand right in this spot," she insists through gritted teeth, "as a reminder of my beloved Isadora, who cannot speak for herself."

The King and Queen exchange a glance, silent communication passing between them. They seem to come to an agreement and the King nods at Veramis. Removing her from the proceedings might cause a riot.

I have ripped the carefully protected peace of the kingdom to shreds, and it will be nearly impossible to repair. All they can do is respect the mother who stands beside me, grieving.

She jerks from the guards' grip, and they glance at their captain nearby, who nods. He cares not about my safety any longer, knowing I am nothing but a deterrent to the royal family who once doted on me. His only concern now is the protection of his sovereigns.

Flustered, his cheeks flushed over the high neck of his coat, Sternbridge motions at the crowd to settle. "Let us watch."

All eyes zero in on the bubble screen, where the faeries still float. One flies to me, tiny as a bee, and waves her wand. A wisp of memory coils from my head, and she returns to the bubble with it.

The hollow ache in my chest grows, my guts twisting as I watch my friend's last moments play out. Her angry words threaten Gretel, another friend who is not in the scene. Izzy launches herself at me, and I raise my hands in defense. Magic explodes around her, and she stumbles, landing inside the raging oven she had stoked the fires of moments before. It's my turn to gasp.

When the replay is over, I stand stunned, unmoving. I remember none of it and can't believe the encounter got so out of hand. "I would never—" The air in my lungs is instantly frozen and cut off from my throat.

"Silence," the Queen demands. Her face, usually so pleasant, so perfect in its beauty, is enraged. I claw at my throat as she stands and walks down from her throne to stare me in the eyes. "You have violated the most sacred of the peace treaty covenants. The most sacred in our *world*. There is no excuse, no justification for this."

She's right—there isn't. I bow my head, wondering if this is how I'll die, suffocating at her feet. I can't even speak to argue, nor can I offer my regrets and apologies again.

Sick at all of this, I search the far reaches of the room, shocked to see my godmother watching everything play out. A known Outcast, it is against the rules for her to be here. Her beloved sword, Gunther, is in hand, her thumb idly scraping over the edge of the blade without it harming her.

The restriction on my lungs eases, and I suck in air. I wonder if Marlena, then, has been granted a pardon to enact my punishment.

Unable to bear the disappointment on her face, I scan the crowd for my friends. The argument was over Gretel, but she's not in attendance. There is no one to come to my defense or even offer support.

Perhaps no one should.

My future, once so promising, is as tattered as my clothes. There is no happily ever after for me.

I imagine a different scenario, where Izzy is alive, and my error is only a silly mistake. I would hear her voice championing me, her magic taking me by my hands and turning us invisible or making me fly. She would laugh as she stole me away from the Throne Room so we could hide in the woods to wait out the Queen's wrath, just like we had so many times before.

My heart's aching eases remembering times when we defied our parents' expectations and our realm's norms, Izzy leading me on a merry path of teenage rebellion.

But those days are over, and my lungs are filled with frost. Even as I inhale deeply, my final act of rebellion is over.

A male voice shouts from the open doorway. "Your Majesties, I must be heard." Hansel! Hope surges again. "There's more to the story," he insists.

The butterflies disappear as my mother glares at me, the side she rarely shows anyone else surfacing. "There always is with you, isn't there?" She says it under her breath, ignoring him and speaking only to me. My heart sinks. Regardless of what light Gretel's brother might shed on the story, there will be no mercy on this day.

Magic forces my knees to buckle, and I kneel before her. She silences his further protests with a wave of her hand and speaks to me alone. "Princess Ambrosia Seraphina Rothschild of Ever After." Her voice rings clear and true, not a hint of sorrow or dismay. "For your trespasses, you are forever vanquished from our kingdom and realm. You are not to set foot here again for any reason, nor interact with those loyal to the crown. Your position is renounced, and you will no longer be recognized, aided, or granted any kind-ness as one of ours. If you so much as speak to any in humandom of our existence or your heritage, you will imme-diately be struck down by the sword of justice."

It's not the beheading or fiery end I anticipated, yet the ramifications make me stagger. I can barely speak over a whisper. "You would renounce your own daughter?"

Her silver eyes are without compassion. The kingdom's fate rests on her shoulders and will always come before me. "Remove her from my presence," she commands the captain of the guards. "See that she is exiled to the human world, now and forevermore."

Chapter Two

The portal makes an ugly belch as it spews me from Ever After into the world of humans and dumps me on my backside.

Here—wherever on Earth *here* is—it's night, and the sky pours rain. There's a blaring honk, and two matching lights blind me. I instinctively roll to the side, snapping my fingers to create a protective shield. My magic fizzles in the foggy air, nothing but dull sparks.

I scramble out of the way, but not before muddy water splashes me, and I somersault over my sodden skirt. When I come to a stop, the back of my head smacks on hard concrete.

Perfect. I'm wet, sooty, and blood-streaked, and my gown is in tatters. On top of that, my head now throbs with an intensity that makes my eyes water. The cast iron lamp looming over me blurs, becoming three. My vision does not clear as I blink—is it from the rain or the growing lump on the back of my skull? Massaging it gently, I grimace and shut my eyes for the briefest of moments, shivering.

It's far too chilly and wet to lie here. I roll onto my side, fighting the vertigo that strikes. A strand of hair falls in front of my face, and I gasp, sitting up too quickly at the sight of the snowy white tress.

My hair! I blink again, realizing my skin, too, is stripped of color. It is as pale as my mother's favored milky-pink roses.

Is this why my magic has failed me? Did coming through the portal rob me of it, along with my normal coloring?

As is my nature, I search for a comforting thought. *At least I'm free of the manacles.*

Pulse beating like a hummingbird's wings, I reach inside my pocket and locate the tiny candy toadstools. One cap is red with white dots—a strawberry. The other is a cheery yellow—lemon. I wish to eat both, but I have nothing besides my clothes and these two pieces of candy. Best to conserve them until I can make more.

"Cars," a hovering ghost says to me. "That's what humans call them."

I jump up. Another vehicle passes and I stumble farther from the curb, avoiding the rooster tail of dirty water this time. The action seems pointless with the rain falling and my current mess.

Swinging my head wildly, I search for the phantom. He's gone. I tell myself it's only stress getting to me—I do *not* see spirits. Never have. Only those in the Black Heart Court trifle with such magic.

As the retreating taillights vanish, I wipe my face and fling water from the ends of my fingers. My hair lies flat against my forehead. Rivulets of rain run into my eyes, and I wipe them away to clear my vision again.

The sky is a tangle of heavy, roiling clouds and shadows. My heart feels the same, my mother's decree ringing in my ears. *Exiled*.

I am *Outcast*.

At least my godmother didn't have to behead me.

Positive thoughts—that's what I must hold on to.

An owl screeches, and I turn in his direction. "I feel your pain," I call. "By chance, do you know the way to a dry abode and warm fire?"

His reply is the flap of wings. Once above the skeletal trees, he screeches what sounds like a warning, although I cannot translate it. My ability to understand the animal kingdom's languages must also be gone. Or perhaps, even in the kingdom of humans, the Queen's proclamation holds dominion—I am not to be aided.

Taking stock of my surroundings, I avoid thinking overly much about the fact my mother has disowned me, my magic is gone, and I have murdered my best friend.

Oh, Izzy. The memory pulled from my head still seems... wrong. We had argued plenty of times, but she would never yell at me so. Never attack me with such rage in her eyes.

Would she?

Even in self-defense, would I shove her into my oven?

Never. I know this as sure as I know my name.

The satin fabric of my gown plasters itself to my legs, and reddish clay coats my slippers. A bubble of panic starts below my rib cage. "Can anyone assist me?" I call into the gloom.

There are no lights from homes, only a glistening road

disappearing into the fog. I have no sense of direction, and although I am a faery tale witch—and a princess to boot—I know humans are not known for accepting the magical and supernatural. They revel in morbid curiosity about it, yet if their fascination with such a thing were to materialize, they would run screaming the other way.

"Follow the road."

It's another specter, and I jump before I pinch my lips into a line so I do not cry out as I watch her vanish into the woods. "Wait!"

No one else answers my request, neither human, Fae, nor animal. Only the rain keeps me company as I follow her advice.

I must find a way forward, not only to discover shelter but to determine what I will do in the years that stretch in front of me, devoid of friends, my family, and my former life.

In Ever After, the only way a princess might meet her end is through a poisoned apple or an unfortunate accident. Here, who knows? I may be as mortal as the humans who occupy this realm.

A bleak resignation takes hold. I rest a hand on my belly, where it is unsettled. As the crown princess of the land of faery tales, I have never wanted for anything, least of all aid.

"Well," I say aloud, my voice shaky from my chattering teeth. "I may be exiled, and my magic may be inert, but I'm not without intelligence and reason." It's vain of me, but I briefly touch my face and release a relieved breath. While my hair and skin are bleached of their natural color, I seem to have my beauty, which can be used for leverage here.

Unless *I'm* a phantom. The sheer idea brings me to a complete stop. Is that why I can now see and hear them?

I shudder violently and have to breathe in and out several times to assure myself I am alive. Rallying, I begin walking again, more determined than ever to figure this out. "Nobody can strip my birthright from me," I mutter. "Not even the Queen."

Magic *does* exist here; I need to find a way to tap into it. If there is a way forward, and I believe there is, it begins with me relying on what makes me *me*.

I am Princess Ambrosia Rothschild of Ever After. A good witch who makes the sweetest candies the fae world has ever tasted. I may never take the throne, never rule, but royal blood runs in my veins, and I can recreate my confections anywhere.

Giving in to my craving, I pop a toadstool into my mouth. Instantly soothed, I suck on it as I contemplate what to do. The lemon cap gives me a sugar rush and calms my nerves, but it does nothing to stave off the cold. Goose flesh rises on my arms, and I rub them and move faster to warm the regal blood I carry.

There are others like me. Outcasts from Ever After. The name itself is considered foul to us, a curse. Yet, I know none of those exiled here if Marlena has returned to her former status in the kingdom. I've heard they rarely fare well in this realm. They, along with the native-born supernaturals, make themselves blend in for fear of subjugation from the humans in power.

Regardless of my pep talk, loneliness slips under my damp skin. When I see lights in the distance and hear the grumble of more cars, I am unsure if the wetness on my cheeks is from the rain or my tears.

A one-story building with square windows and lighted

signs announcing *Lottery* and *Marlboro $7.19* comes into view. A man stands out front, a hose running from a gas tank to his car. He talks on a handheld phone.

"Fair night," I call, even though it is anything but. I raise a hand in greeting. "Where might I find lodging, perhaps dry clothes and food?"

He narrows his eyes at my appearance and speaks into the phone. "I gotta call you back." He pockets the device and disengages the hose from his vehicle. "You lost, little lady?"

I am that. I stop and smile through the rain running down my face. The pungent smell of gasoline hangs in the air, making my nose itch. A trace of something else is there, too, but I can't place it. "I find myself in need of your generosity. I am definitely in an unfamiliar territory."

The return smirk he offers makes my skin crawl. "Is that so?"

Onyx, my beloved gargoyle pendant, heats in warning where he lays on my collarbone.

I back away, automatically searching for my magic to tell me what type of candy he is. Then I remember it's gone.

Black licorice, I guess.

A child-like being in the car's back seat leans its face against the window. The overly large head, hooked nose, and flat gaze causes me to tense. It's not human, although it probably appears to be to the non-magical.

It smiles, and three rows of teeth gleam at me. Sharp, pointed teeth.

That smell... I recognize it now. I choke, then fumble in the folds of my skirt for the toadstool. "Here." I hold it out to the man as he stalks toward me. "For you."

His brows dip, confused and questioning.

"It's strawberry," I say, wiggling it in front of his nose. I do not sense he is anything but human, but I need to get away from him. This is the only distraction I can come up with.

He takes it reluctantly and reaches for my wrist at the same time. I dodge his grip and whirl.

Through the rain-streaked window, a woman behind the counter peers at us. My presence has caught her attention. I point toward the glass door, where I spot rows of wrapped candy. I could use one—or maybe twelve. "I believe what I need is inside. I'll leave you to your night. Fair thee well."

"Hold on there." He's suddenly beside me. A rough hand grabs my elbow and jerks me around. "Thought you wanted my help."

Vexation at his rudeness causes my voice to come out low and dangerous. "Remove your hand this instant."

While I may be a princess, I am not helpless. When he tries to force me toward his car, I stomp on the top of his foot. He curses, shoving me away and hopping about like a chicken.

My grin turns triumphant, and the door to the building opens. A small bell dings. "Is there a problem out here?" the woman calls.

I hustle toward her, exhaling with relief once I'm inside. "I'm afraid I'm lost and in need of direction. Perhaps you could assist me?"

Her eyes are the color of smoky quartz and match her smooth skin. They sweep over me as the door shuts softly on its own. She glares at the man, but he has already returned to his vehicle. He can't smell the entity in his car nor see its true visage. To him, it appears an innocent human child.

She points to a sign over a wooden door on my left that reads *Women*. "You can clean up in there. If he tries anything, I'll call the po-po."

"The what?"

She scans my clothes. "You're not from around here, are you?"

"Afraid not." Understanding clicks in my brain. "He will no longer be a problem. No need to call anyone."

She makes a noise in her throat that seems to be agreement. If I had to guess—which I do since my magic is gone —I'd say she loves chocolate, any and all varieties.

I immediately like her.

After I've cleaned the mud from my slippers to the best of my non-magical abilities, and dried my face, I return to the main floor. She is speaking to someone on a phone attached to the wall behind the counter. This device has a long, kinked-up cord and is dingy with handprints. She holds it to her ear, using her shoulder as she simultaneously eyes the customer at the counter.

"We do not require law enforcement," a familiar voice says. "Please disconnect your call."

My godmother's compulsion magic mesmerizes the smoky-eyed woman, and she does as instructed. Marlena is in her fighting leathers rather than a customary gown. Gunther, at her hip, vibrates at my nearness, alerting her. She pivots, taking me in. I sob with joy as I throw myself at her.

She accepts my hug and returns it fiercely. "There you are." She frowns at my hair and complexion. "What happened to you?"

The portal has stripped her of nothing. "I'm not sure, but perhaps the Queen marked me somehow? Pray tell she didn't exile you again for my crime." I fear I have indeed condemned her. It is the only explanation for her presence. "I saw you in Ever After. She granted you pardon?"

Her silver and black curls are tight as springs, quivering when she shakes her head. "We were in talks about it." She chucks my chin as a siren wails in the distance. "After the sentencing, I turned down the offer and petitioned your parents to give me leave to follow you."

I am astounded, not only at her request but that they granted it. Perhaps they still care about me and have sent her to be a guide, even though my sentence forbids it. "That you would do so is something I can never repay. What of the realm? Will the citizenry not see that as a violation of the terms of my exile?"

She winks, eyes filled with mischief. "It is our secret. Besides, everyone knows my status as Outcast. Your parents will continue the facade of caring nothing about either of us, and the kingdom will forget us in time."

The surprises of this day keep coming. Exhaustion creeps into my bones.

Marlena flicks a hand at a shelf of pastries nearby. "You need sugar, but not that garbage."

"Hey." Ire, over the criticism, upsets the clerk, even though she had nothing to do with creating them.

Blue lights cut through the windows, and my godmother grabs my hand. "Time for us witches to fly. This is no place for us."

I try to call up my magic, but it is still missing. I snap my fingers, and all that happens is a dull spark. That's more than what I could conjure in the restroom, but it's not enough. "It's gone. My magic is...dead." Just like my friend. "I can't remember what happened with Izzy. I know what the memory showed, but..."

"Your magic isn't dead, just in shock, and you probably are, too. It's screwing up your memory. I know you, and I know you would never murder anyone. Something is wrong with the whole situation, but we'll worry about that later. Physics works differently on this plane. This is a place of science and logic, laws such as gravity. Those, rather than magic, hold domain here." She waves a hand, and I am covered in glittering faery dust. My soiled gown transforms into a vibrant raspberry dress with a matching cape. My wet slippers become black leather boots that reach up past my knees. I touch my hair, dry and braided, and giggle.

She eyes her handiwork. "You'll learn the rules that govern this world, and soon, you will blend in with the mundanes. I promise. They'll love you."

I'm reassured. My language, style of dress, and mannerisms will soon appear as human as the chocolate-loving woman staring in shock at us.

Two men in dark blue uniforms rush inside, and she cocks her head toward us. One is about to lay hands on me when my godmother blinks.

We are instantly transported through space and time, no portal necessary.

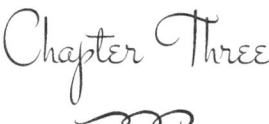

Chapter Three

All great faery tales involve wicked witches, handsome princes, and damsels in distress.

While humans prefer those that end with a happily ever after, not all do. As I let magic whisk me to a safer place, I wonder which mine will end with.

I once more land in the path of bright lights and pouring rain, but strong arms sweep me up before the car can run me over. In a heartbeat, I am deposited safely on the side of the road.

"Why, hello," a deep, husky voice says. The creature it comes from is tall, dark, and deliciously dangerous, if the magic coming off him is any indication. "What an unexpected pleasure to find you on my path."

I'm never at a loss for words, but my tongue feels as if I've sucked on too many hot cinnamons. "Um, fair evening."

His hands continue to steady me, and I feel light as a feather as I stare into eyes that are the deepest obsidian. He gives the slightest bow. "It is that."

"Thank you for..." I cannot bring myself to say *rescuing me.* "For your timely intervention."

Around us, passersby glance our way. There is a goddess wearing a toga, a cowboy in leathers, and a witch in a tight, short dress that shows an enormous amount of skin. Her boots are similar to mine.

Tall, dark, and dangerous appears oblivious to them. He wears a black wool coat with shiny silver buttons. His hair is perfectly coiffed, and there is no sign that the rain has touched him. "Whatever were you doing in the middle of the intersection?"

Tearing my gaze away, I search the area. It would not do for me to lose my godmother after she has just found me. "I didn't see the carriage—I mean, car."

Marlena is climbing out of a large urn of mums, soggy blooms sticking to her suit. Surrounding the base of the planter are jack-o'-lanterns and hay bales. She steps down on a pumpkin, half smashing it, and stumbles. Even her magic is affected by the physics of this dimension. "Apologies, Prin —" she stops herself before divulging my name. "My aim was off."

The creature, who looks like a man but moves too swiftly and exudes preternatural stillness, doesn't so much as glance her way. He only stares at me. "Are you okay?"

The noise of the cars zooming past fades into the background. I hear the patter of rain, but the two of us are dry. We are under a bubble. A magic bubble. Outside of it, it is indeed still drizzling. "I am well, thank you."

It's clear I'm not, but he doesn't point that out. As my godmother joins us, his bubble encompasses her as well. He takes in our attire. "Are you on your way to the costume party?"

Parties have plenty of food and drink. Just what we need. "Um...yes...?" I am always up for frivolity; right now, we need to blend in until we figure out a plan. I wish I hadn't wasted my last candy cap on that rude man at the gas station. "But we've gotten ourselves turned around. Could you point us in the right direction?"

Marlena gives a chastising grunt. "We need no help."

The stranger arches a brow as if in question.

"Yes, we do." I give Marlena a version of my mother's quelling glare. Then, I shower the male before me with a glorious Ever After smile. "And we would be in your debt if you could offer some."

Magic or no, I can still charm and enchant. He blinks, smitten, and the corners of his mouth quirk up ever so slightly. "I'm Torren." He holds out an arm for me to take. "I'm attending the party and would consider it an honor to escort you two lovely ladies."

I flutter my lashes and don't miss Marlena's eye roll. I've never been a flirt in my entire enchanted life, but it seems appropriate now. Accepting his arm, I touch Onyx at my neck, signaling to Marlena that we are not in danger.

Although she knows I am in no way a simpering female, I can see by the flare of her nostrils that she is concerned I may be under the influence of the sexy male and his magic. The scent of it *is* delicious, an intoxicating blend of my favorite cognac and caramel flavorings.

Throughout Ever After, they knew me far and wide for my sweetness. Part of my magic, it enriches my celebrated candies as much as my countenance and gentle words. Here, however, I may need a layer of tenacity and cautiousness under my natural desire to trust everyone at face value.

Izzy's nefarious smile flashes in my mind as if I've conjured her. She would have found this male delectable and immediately played his game, pretending to be under his spell only to turn it around on him and drag him under hers.

I'm not one for such games, but I know males love food. I wonder which of my creations he would most enjoy—if he eats at all. While Ever After has no such beings like him, I believe I know what he is. I hate to admit it, but I *am* a damsel in distress, and he is a handsome princeling—even if it may be one of the night.

I channel Izzy. "Torren, you are a knight in shining armor." I don't offer my name but motion at the path. "We would be delighted with your company."

He smiles, and his magic hits me full force. His true nature is revealed—literally.

Fangs. He has *fangs*.

I have indeed fallen in league with a vampyre. Will the surprises of this day never end?

Marlena slips her arm through my free one. "Where exactly is this party?"

I feel like I'm the rope in a tug of war as the three of us journey down the sidewalk. My senses reel at the feel of Torren's solid arm under my hand and his irresistible scent. The confections I could create with cognac and caramel...

"Enchanted Haven," he says. The rain has ceased entirely, and only then do I realize the streets are decorated for autumn as if it is the most wondrous season of all. Every doorway and window has pumpkins, mums, skeletons, and black cats. Dried corn stalks and sunflowers are tied to lamp-posts, and orange, yellow, and red lights spiderweb over bushes. "I love Halloween!"

This seems to please him. "It's the annual festival. A full month of celebrations, ending on the holiday itself."

Indeed. Everywhere I look, I see humans and non-enjoying themselves. We have crossed some invisible line, and the streets are dry; the trees lining the walkways are covered with brightly colored leaves.

There is a large stone well in the center of a roundabout. It must be six feet in circumference. Moss covers the sides of the ancient stones, and ivy winds around the upright beams holding the bucket. As I watch, the rim of the wide opening seems to glow.

Torren sees my fascination. "The Witching Well. The town was built around it."

I'm drawn to it, my feet seeming to have a mind of their own. "Witching, not wishing?"

"Magic workers founded our town." He winks. "They liked the pun."

Marlena stops me with a hand. "Good or evil, these witches?"

He fishes a coin from his pocket, the gold gleaming under the streetlights. The silvery buttons on his coat do as well. "Good, I assure you. This place is a refuge, a sanctuary, for all misunderstood creatures born of magic."

"I love wishes," I utter, running a hand over the old stones. They are alive with the power of those who created the structure and the thousands of hopes and desires of those who've used it. It soaks into my palm, warm and enticing.

"Go ahead." He hands me the coin. "Make one. What do you dream of making come true?"

So many things. Impossible things. The metal is warm in my palm, and I turn the coin over and over between my fingers.

"Make it a good one," Marlena growls.

I think of my family, of the friend I lost due to my horrible actions. Can a wish turn back time? Keep those I love safe and deliver me from making a terrible and tragic mistake?

I know there is no magic that powerful. *Keep it simple*, I tell myself, even though it feels as though so much is riding on it.

Raising the gold to my lips, I kiss it, close my eyes, and cast. For long seconds, the metal drops, drops, drops, turning end over end as I watch, and finally—*splash*.

The ground trembles, or perhaps it's simply my knees. Magic, sure and true, rushes over me. The tiny hairs on my arms lift, my toes curl. I taste sweetness laced with a bitter aftertaste on my tongue. I wonder what I have done, but know it—like time—is too late to call back.

When I turn to Torren and Marlena, both stare at me with wide eyes.

"What the broomsticks was that?" my godmother asks. "What did you wish for?"

"You know I can't share that." I give her a chastising glare. "The rules are the rules." Everyone knows you must keep a wish secret, or it won't come true. "It would be to your liking if it were to pass, so wipe the scowl off your face. You'll acquire wrinkles."

A brow rises with her temper. "Take care of your tongue, or I will cut it out."

Torren watches our exchange, and his lips twitch again. He offers me his arm once more. "Shall we?"

With a wink at her, I link mine through his. "We certainly shall."

Chapter Four

Young and old alike are out in droves. They stream from store to store, sipping from pumpkin-shaped mugs and laughing as they carry shopping bags. Some are dressed in costumes; others, like our companion, are free to be themselves.

Curiosity and caution war with each other as I observe the scene. "The humans don't realize that you and the other magic-wielders are real?"

He pats my hand. "A few. They keep the knowledge to themselves. You'll fit right in."

Relief warms me. We pass a store with no lights and no decorations. It looks sad in comparison to the rest. A crooked sign in the window advertises the building is for sale. "Why is this empty?"

"The former candy shop? The human who owned it eloped and ran off. No one has seen or heard from her since."

"How romantic."

Marlena's eye roll is so dramatic that I'm surprised she doesn't tip over. "Her husband probably killed her."

So much for romance.

"The place has been empty a long time," Torren says, "and the town council had to put it up for sale. A few have looked at it, but..."

When he doesn't finish, I must ask, "But what?"

"Some think the original owners haunt the place."

Ghosts, great. At least I haven't seen any since my arrival. A seed of an idea forms. "Do the citizens here like candy?"

Marlena pinches my arm. Not hard, but in caution. "You can't be serious," she murmurs under her breath.

Oh, but I am. "Serious as chocolate-covered cherries."

"You have no capital," she reminds me.

Hmm.

The vampyre nods. "Doesn't everyone love candy? Are you a baker?"

"I am, indeed," I tell him. "My treats are quite famous."

"Torren," a man calls from the steps of a building in the square. The double-door entrance is open, inviting lights behind him. Although he's backlit, I see his long hair, keen eyes, and broad chest. He's dressed from head to toe in black, and the scent of were-being floats on the air as we draw near. "You're late."

"A beautiful distraction kept me from my schedule," our host says, guiding us up the stone steps. "Cynric, meet..." He turns to me. "I'm afraid I didn't catch your name."

Onyx warms slightly, coaching my response. I glance at the were-being, probably a wolf from the alpha posture he exhibits and the long hair secured at the nape of his neck. With a glance back, I take in the view of the town from this vantage point. The entire place bubbles with happiness.

I *was* Princess Ambrosia of Ever After. Here, that means little. I need to reinvent myself and create my own faery tale. "Seraphina," I say. "Rothschild." Close enough. "And this is my godmother, Marlena." I nod at her. Her glare could melt lemon drops. "We were unexpectedly caught in a downpour and became turned around. Torren gallantly came to our aid."

"That's Tor for you. Mr. Gallant." The beast pats the vampyre's back. It earns him a pointed look. "I'm Cyn, the town preacher and funeral director. Come on. Let's get you ladies a drink."

Torren manages to elbow him in the stomach as we pass into the great room, but the werewolf laughs it off. People mill about, laughter and chatter drifting over upbeat music. There is a dance floor and tables filled with food and punch. A reflective ball spins above it all, sending beams of colored lights over us. It's quite entrancing, and several people speak to Torren as he leads us to the punch bowl.

Picking up the conversation again, he hands me a cup of pink liquid. "You could get a loan, without collateral, from the Chamber, I bet. The council frowns on empty store-fronts, and they would gladly give lenient terms."

Marlena accepts hers next but doesn't drink. I see her mind working behind her guarded expression. She is clever and knows more about this world than I do. "What kind of strings would be attached?"

"Strings?" I echo. "You mean compensation? I could provide them with pastries each morning, and I'm a candy connoisseur. They could have first dibs on any confections I make. Would that be sufficient exchange?"

Torren's look is quizzical, and he chuckles. "You aren't from around here, are you?"

His words echo that of the chocolate-loving woman, and I bite my bottom lip and turn away. What can I do to make it less obvious?

Another supernatural male approaches, cowboy boots stomping on the wooden floor. His magic tingles my skin. "What's this I hear about candy bribes?"

"Seraphina and Marlena,"—Torren motions from us to him—"meet Mayor Jo. Joseph, these ladies are interested in the old candy shop."

"Is that so?" The touch of his hand is otherworldly when we shake. How accurate is his hearing since he was nowhere in sight when I mentioned candy? I've never encountered this type of being and nearly blurt out a rude question that would surely put him on the spot.

Marlena is there to engage him first, saving me from a blunder. "If it's up for discussion, we'd like to negotiate terms."

"There hasn't been any interest in the place for months." A spark of hope lights his pale blue eyes. I bet he likes coffee-flavored truffles and decadent angel food cake. "If you can make good on the pastries and candy, I'll give you the keys Monday morning."

Marlena sips and eyes him. "No formal agreement? That's not how we do business."

"Don't worry—I won't let you take advantage of me." He winks, and she splutters. "Swing by my office at Haven Hall after the party, and we'll draw up the papers."

Could it be so easy? "We'll do that," I say before my godmother can argue.

He offers a mock bow to her, and she turns a shade of pink I've never seen on her golden skin. It matches the punch. A police officer I recognize from the gas station rushes up. "Mayor, we have a situation."

I turn away, hoping he doesn't recognize me. My chest tightens like a vise.

The mayor is instantly serious. "What is it, Canton?"

"Might be best if I show you." He gestures at an exit.

My ribcage loosens, and I take a deep breath as they walk off. "Definitely angel food cake," I mutter.

"What was that?" Torren asks.

"Nothing." I suck down my drink. *Ah, sugar.* "Do you happen to like cognac?"

"I have a glass every night."

"Caramels, too?"

He turns perplexed. "How did you know?"

My magic is awaking once more. Marlena and I exchange a smile. "One of my skills," I tell him, feeling satisfied.

"You are a very...interesting." His focus goes to my white hair, my porcelain skin. "I'm unsure what exactly you are. Not human. Not vampyre. Not zombie."

"Goodness, no." But I don't offer to fill in the blank that hangs between us.

This piques his curiosity even more. He holds out a hand. "Care to dance?"

Marlena pulls me away. "Not tonight. Nice meeting you. We have to go."

"We do not," I argue.

She juts her chin at a group of men striding inside. "Yes, we do."

Mayor Jo leads the procession, and now both officers from the gas station are with him. They are all looking at me.

"Oh." My happiness deflates. "I didn't do anything," I tell Torren. "No matter what they claim. I swear on my mint chocolate meltaways."

"Seraphina?" Mayor Jo calls.

"Now," Marlena says, and I feel her releasing her magic. She grabs my hand, and I drop the punch.

The plastic cup hits the floor, and liquid splashes my boots. Torren grabs my other hand as if desperate to keep me from fleeing. The music has died, and the partygoers stare. "What happened?"

It's too late to fly now. "I've done nothing wrong," I insist to Marlena. My royal blood has awakened with my powers. My voice comes out strong. "Stand down."

Instantly, she releases me. Torren does not.

"What is it, mayor?" I ask with pure innocence in my tone.

"That's her," one of the officers says. He's holding a piece of paper. "She was at the convenience store where the guy bought gas. The clerk called us, but these two vanished before we could question them."

I feign confusion. "Is that against your laws? Disappearing?"

Torren smirks. Mayor Jo frowns. "Could you step out back with us and identify a body? I'm afraid it isn't pretty, and normally, I wouldn't ask such a thing, but he lacks identification. We believe you may know him."

Marlena is already moving toward the back exit. "A body? What happened to him?"

"Another murder?" Torren asks at the same time.

The two exchange a glance.

The mayor gestures for them to lower their voices. He forces a smile and waves at those gawking at us. "Everything's fine, folks. Munson? Get that music going. Everybody enjoy the dance."

The music cranks up again.

"How can we help?" Marlena is all business. She loves a good mystery, but murder? I want to stay as far as possible from such a thing, especially after what happened in Ever After.

"Come with me," Major Jo says, leading the way.

I'm forced to follow. The music grows muted, and the night closes in as we step outside, only the illumination from a pair of flashlights to guide us.

It is indeed the man who accosted me. He bears ragged teeth marks on his neck and chest. The blood is still wet and shines under the lights. I turn away and put a hand to my mouth.

"It's graphic," the mayor says, "and I apologize twelve times over, but do you recognize him?"

I swallow and nod. It is not the blood and gore that makes me squeamish. "He spoke to me at the station," I say, and catch Marlena's eyes as she turns them on me. "But I don't know him."

As if I've conjured the man's ghost, I feel a frigid wave of air sweep over me. A filmy gray version of him hovers close, looking down on himself. "You did this," he snarls at me.

"I did not," I say without thinking.

"Didn't what?" The mayor asks.

"Um," I falter, glaring at the ghost. "Didn't like him very much. He grabbed me and tried to force me into his car."

The phantom curses.

None of my companions realize he's there, and I try to convince myself I'm hallucinating.

"And this?" Mayor Jo takes one of the flashlights and shines it in the man's open mouth. "It appears the killer left a calling card."

Marlena, already on to the fact that she and I know very well what kind of creature has done this, notices what he's spotlighting, gapes, and fixes her attention on me. "What in the once upon a time...?"

"This may seem an odd question," the mayor continues, "but have you ever seen anything like this, Ms. Rothschild?"

It's not odd at all after our recent discussion about candies and the fact I volunteered that the man assaulted me.

For in his open mouth is the very candy mushroom I gave him.

Chapter Five

A mouse scampers into the square cell where I reside. *It's for your own good*, the mayor told me before locking me away.

I know better—thanks to my candy, I've become his number one suspect. The fact Torren told him I smelled of the man...and of blood added to his suspicions.

"Never trust a vampyre," Marlena had whispered in my ear as they snapped the cuffs on. Once more, I found myself in manacles.

The mouse is coated in faery dust. I bend down to look him in the eye. "Did Marlena send you, my tiny friend?"

He hops onto the cot and then my lap, where he shakes himself. Snowflakes of glittering dust fly over me.

"Ooh," a ghost says in a wavering, high-pitched voice. She hovers several feet off the floor, watching the dust in the low light, her ankle-length skirt moving as if there's a breeze. "Can I have some?"

"Help yourself," I tell her, noting the gashes across her

neck. It's irrefutable—I now see and talk to the dead. "Did you die in here?"

She reaches out to trap a few specks of dust between her fingers. "My cell mate. She didn't like my singing, and she had sharp nails."

"Is there no way for you to...you know." What do humans call it? "Move on?"

"Move on to what?" She tastes the dust. "It's like snowflakes on your tongue. So sweet."

It does taste like sugar. I have never eaten snowflakes, but I'm sure I would like them if they taste sweet. "What's your name?"

"Heloise, but I hate that name. I prefer Flower."

"How lovely." She begins twirling, arms outstretched. I grow dizzy watching. "Do you know of any way I can get out of here? Any secret tunnels or hidden implements I could use to break through the walls?"

"I'm freeeee," she says, throwing her head back. "This is some hallucinogen. Whee!"

Have I drugged the poor ghost? "Flower? Maybe you should—"

She vanishes.

"That's unfortunate." Or maybe not. I pet my warm friend, still alive and cuddling in my lap. If only the bars weren't iron. I cannot touch them, must less attempt to squeeze through them. Fae and iron don't mix. "I'm afraid the bars of this place keep me from escape," I explain to him, "even *with* magic. Tell my godmother I am as well as can be expected, and I will find a way to convince the mayor of my innocence."

A strong wave of vampyre magic rolls over me, and the

mouse scurries off, disappearing into the shadows once more. "Perhaps I can help with that." Torren appears, holding a lidded cup and white bag. "Refreshments."

He passes them through the bars, but I turn up my nose. I can't blame him for telling the truth to the mayor, but it is part of the reason I'm trapped here. "That's the best you can do as a peace offering?"

"I know you didn't kill the man. The scent of his blood doesn't match the one that was on you. At first, I thought it did since you smelled of him, but going over the scene again, I noted differences."

My stomach rumbles, yearning to eat whatever is inside that bag. I edge close to the bars to look him in the eye. "Did you tell Mayor Jo this? If so, why am I still locked in here?"

He extends his offering through the bars. "You really should keep your strength up."

I check the bag's contents, the aroma of yeast and sugar filling my nose. The treat is hardly fresh, nor is it to my liking. I shove the gift back at him, the bag crumpling as I press it against his chest.

His solid, impressive chest.

His fingers brush mine as he takes it. "Our illustrious mayor is correct—it's safer for you here. The murderer will believe he's off the hook, and that will give me a chance to track him down."

"So you didn't tell Mayor Jo I'm innocent?"

"We need proof, and I will get it. I'm skilled in solving such issues."

Frustrated, I ignore the intensity of his gaze and his wickedly delicious magic that teases mine. "I don't doubt your abilities, but when it comes to scenting our target, would not a shifter be more suited to tracking him?"

He grins, and I feel it down to my toes. "Don't trust me, princess?"

Princess. I swallow hard. Does he know, or is the moniker an innocuous term, like 'dear' or 'sweetie?' "I had hoped you came to help me escape." I huff a sigh and return to my seat.

The corner of his mouth quirks. "That is my intent."

Bewildered, I try not to fall under his mesmerizing gaze. Those eyes... "Is this a vampyre thing—confusing your prey before you attack?"

His brows furrow, and he sets the bag and cup on the concrete floor inside the bars. "Why would I attack you?"

"It's what your kind do, isn't it?" I shake my head and rub my eyes. "This realm is puzzling. If you came here for a purpose other than to bring me weak coffee and a stale donut, please state it."

"This *realm*?" His features turn canny. "I knew it. You're *not* from here."

"Neither is the killer. We need to focus on him. *It*."

"As we shall." The mouse scurries from his hiding place to knock over the bag and drag out the pastry. "I have a plan, if you're game, to flush him out and clear your name."

I'll do anything to stop the killer—a kobold from the Black Heart Court—and be released from this dreary confinement, but I sense there is a price to be paid for working with him. A price that sends shivers over my skin. I clear my throat and reluctantly break eye contact. "I'm sure my godmother will take care of this misunderstanding."

His expensive suit rustles softly as he grips the bars. An

emerald ring flashes in the dim light. "About that. I'm afraid she's disappeared."

I shoot to my feet, dread filling my belly. The mouse races off, clutching the pastry that is as big as he is. "*What*?"

"As soon as you were taken into custody, she vanished. I searched but could not detect her trail. Is it possible she has gone to apprehend the killer alone?"

Undoubtedly, yes, she left to hunt down the kobold, but what if...

I move as close as I dare, searching his face for any hint of deception. I find none. "What is this plan?"

His beautiful eyes glance up at the camera mounted in the corner. I feel a slight push against my mind and hear his voice inside my head. *It would be best to pretend to fall asleep and do exactly as I say. I'll explain everything once we're outside.*

To trust him or not...it could be the most important question of my life. Marlena's words ring in my head, *never trust a vampyre*. Onyx warms, but only slightly—a warning that the plan will put me in danger or that Torren will?

My skin sparkles from the dust, and I wonder who could have sent it if not for my godmother. Is it a tool to help me escape or a missive for help?

So many questions. My mind buzzes with them. Marlena can dispatch a single kobold, but there could be more. In Ever After, they hang out in packs, pretending to be children in order to trick others. A horde of them, living here, doing as they please and tormenting these people... murdering them? I shudder at the thought of her falling into their grasp. The one from earlier has used my candy against me.

Acting exhausted isn't a stretch of my acting skills. I yawn and blink several times. This could be a mistake, yet freedom is my first and foremost priority. I'll figure out how much to trust Torren once I'm out. "I'm afraid I need to rest," I say loudly. "Please leave."

I lay on the cot and fake sleep, waiting for the creature on the other side of the bars to do something.

I keep waiting. Nothing happens.

I peek open an eye. He has disappeared.

What trickery is this?

I'm about to sit up and growl my frustration when shadows emerge from every corner, enveloping me, the floor, the ceiling—everything. What has he done? I gulp, fear racing through me.

They enclose me in a new type of cage—I'm entirely blind.

Chapter Six

The door squeaks ever so slightly, and I feel strong hands lifting me from the cot.

"Hurry," I hear Torren say close to my ear, even though I cannot see him. I can't see *anything*. "I've glamoured you and the cell. No one will see us leave."

Being blind is daunting, yet he guides me through the night he has created. Freedom beckons, and my heart responds. Lifting my skirt, I allow his urgent tug to lead the way.

Shortly, I'm breathing in damp air, relieved to leave behind the intense blindness. Stars twinkle overhead, and Torren materializes before me, the last shadows slinking off. I let loose a shaky laugh as we pause in the alley behind City Hall and withdraw my hand from his. "How did you do that?"

"Magic." He grins. "I suspect from the light in your eyes that you enjoyed that."

A return grin tugs at my mouth. I try to force it away,

but it breaks free. "Breaking out of jail? It's quite a new experience for me."

"You like being daring and taking risks, don't you?"

I chuckle. Adrenaline is as fine of a mood lifter as sugar, and there is plenty coursing through me at the moment. "I've always had to follow the rules, the protocols. My friend, Izzy—" I abruptly shut my mouth, guilt, pain, and sorrow flooding me.

"Is it her blood I scented on you?"

Biting my lip, I nod. "She's the daring one. *Was*, I mean." I force a smile. "She had a knack for getting me into trouble." There's a wistfulness in my voice I can't suppress. "She would have liked you."

His stare is as dark and intense as the shadows he summoned. "I'd like to hear more about her. About what happened."

A lump forms in my throat, like I've accidentally swallowed a too-big piece of hard candy. "It's an ugly, complicated story, and I'm not ready to share it."

A dip of his chin. "Just so you know, I'm in no position to judge. Whether you ever discuss it with me or not is your choice; either way, I'm your friend now."

Understanding, a knowingness, flashes in his lovely eyes. He's remembering some atrocity he himself has committed. No one else has looked at me like this, and it means something. Something more than I could have imagined. Only someone who's been through what I have can grasp the depth of emotions I suffer from. Whatever he's done—he *knows* how I feel.

He may be the only one who does.

An odd but powerful bond clicks into place between us.

The lump in my throat softens, and I swallow down my guilt. "Thank you."

We stay like that for another beat of my heart, that silent support comforting. Then he holds out his hand to me. "We should go."

I hesitate, then straighten my spine. The warmth of his skin surprises me again as I slide my fingers into his grasp. It also feels right. Normal. He's my friend. I suppress another grin as we walk quickly. "We find Marlena first. Then the kobold."

"The what?"

"Kobold. They are a nasty bunch. They disguise themselves as children, gain the trust of adults, then murder them. That's who was with the man who attacked me. From the wounds on him, I'm sure the kobold committed the heinous crime."

"I've never heard of them." He hustles me along the alley. A sagging cardboard box is in our path, and a swipe of his hand causes it to fly out of the way, clipping a dumpster. A rat, startled by the noise, runs out, sees us, and darts back into his hiding place under the metal container. "They are common where you come from?"

"They tend to keep to themselves, but yes, they exist there." I need to warn him—they are no ordinary supernatural. He may be a top predator here, but I fear they are still stronger. Just as concerning is the idea he has pretended to be my friend in order to manipulate me into something more than stopping a killer. Yes, I believe he's my friend, but what if Marlena is right? What if I should never trust a vampyre? "Why are you doing this?" I ask, picking my way through the puddles.

"I have my reasons."

Reasons that have to do with our shared understanding or something else? "Tell me."

A beat goes by, and he shakes his head, his body becoming tense. His tone turns cool, demanding. "Not now. It's not your concern."

My feet seem to skip over the paved ground as if the air is urging me along. Friend or not, I don't like being pushed. I tug him to a stop, my magical strength a match for his. "I thought we were friends. Tell me, or I go on alone."

He faces me yet doesn't look me in the eye. "Does it matter?"

"I need to know what your motivation is." Bargains are contracts that cannot be broken in my realm, and I don't like how he's making me feel manipulated. Getting me to let down my guard before he leads me further along a path he seems far too interested in. "It matters a great deal if you're doing this to claim a favor down the road."

Those eyes snap to mine, his face tight. He starts to stay something, stops. The set of his shoulders, along with his reluctance to divulge his motivations, suggests I've guessed correctly—the vampyre has an angle he's playing with this gesture of aid.

Flower pops in, looking him over. "He's cute."

He doesn't see her, raking his free hand over his face, through his hair. His features become unreadable, the dark locks on his head falling back into their roguish placement as if he can't be anything but sexy and perfect. "I assure you I won't call in a favor."

But there is a barrier between us now. I feel it.

"Fine, don't tell me." I release him and start walking. "We're done."

"Oooh, fiery," Flower says, giggling. "Make him chase you. That always works in the movies."

Torren catches me, gently grasping my arm to prevent my escape. "Wait." He sighs heavily, seemingly at war with himself. His voice comes out flat, stony. "My story is ugly and complicated, too."

Flower flaps a ghostly hand. "Drama, drama, drama." She disappears, apparently bored.

I reach for that thread between us. The friendship I was so willing to believe in. All I feel is a wall. He's pushed me out as easily as he drew me in.

I hate it when my godmother is right. "I don't expect you to give up details," I tell him, feeling hollow where I only just felt understood. "I need to ensure there is no pact created between us that I cannot fulfill."

Body tense, he at least offers a nod. "My story is no secret, and I've had no qualms about what occurred until now."

"Why?"

He plunges his hands into his pockets, looks at his feet. "A few months ago, one of my coven members was accused of murdering a mundane. The wounds were consistent with a vampyre attack—at least, that's what I thought then." A cloud skitters across the sky, and I swear I feel the previous shadows creeping up on me. "It was my job to investigate, and I didn't realize there was such a thing as this...this... kobold creature."

"Investigate? Are you law enforcement?"

"A private detective. For supernaturals. Do you have such things in your realm?"

My parents are the judge and jury for serious offenses, and each court has its way of dealing with those who offend the rules. Since we can't tell outright lies, it dispenses with many issues. "We have no need for it."

He flicks his gaze up to my face. "Danika, my closest advisor, pleaded innocent, and I should have believed her. I should have tried harder to prove she was innocent. Instead..."

His remorse latches onto me. There is a deep grief to it that mimics mine over Izzy. "You didn't know. Kobolds are not supposed to enter this realm." I rub my forehead. "This is all very unsettling."

Guilt tangles with regret. Behind that, he's at war over asking me more about my home. He seems to sense I won't tell him and continues. "I had to order her death. It's our law. All the evidence pointed to her, and vampyres who murder mundanes must be dealt with. If not, it would be chaos."

A new lump rises in my throat and refuses to be forced down. I think of my mother letting me off with banishment. It's never easy being a leader. "You're the head of your... coven? You're the king?"

He barks a laugh, then gives a bow. "Master vampyre of the Bane, at your service." Straightening, he continues. "The Bane is my family. They mean everything to me, but I... dislike my role as a leader for the very reason that harming one of them goes against everything in my gut."

The thread between us vibrates, a gentle plucking of truth.

I give a mental sigh of relief, somewhat shocked that I had placed so much weight on it so quickly. The loss of Izzy has left a cavern inside me, and I must be careful of how desperate I am to fill it. "Governing others has many such challenges."

"If it was this kobold, I must know. I must be sure the creature is brought to justice."

To atone for my mistake. He doesn't say it, yet I feel it in my chest. In his eyes, the truth is visible. His motivation is as straightforward as mine, and yet...

I must pull myself out of those soulful eyes before I drown. "There may be more than one. At home, they travel in packs, and I know of no single Outcast who may have made this their territory. Can you pick up a trail?"

"If he can't, I can." Cyn emerges from a darkened doorstep. His hair is tied back, a shadow of a beard sprouting along his chin and across his cheeks. The stubble reflects the moonlight. "How is it you're out of your cell?" His keen eyes turn to my companion.

Torren smiles, showing his fangs. "She's innocent of the crime and knows the true killer. Possibly multiple creatures. I thought it prudent to recruit her help in hunting them down."

Cyn is quiet, his body so still I wonder if he's frozen.

Not frozen, as his chest moves ever so slightly as he breathes, but it's as if he and Torren are sharing telepathy. I feel a bit put out that I'm not included in their mental conversation, especially as I sense it's over me.

Finally, the werewolf's gaze swings my way, something decided between them. "The creature has a unique perfume of death mixed with sweetness. Akin to antifreeze. Any idea which way they might be headed? Would they leave town and lie low?"

"Not if they believe I'm imprisoned for tonight's crime." The shifter reminds me of the lycans in Ever After. They are unfriendly and keep to themselves, primarily residing in the Shadow Kingdom, where the Black Heart Court resides. It seems they feel more at home with those who belong to the night. "They appear to mortals as children, and I'm afraid that on this night, they've most likely been wandering about openly with those who are trick-or-treating. They disguise their malodorous smell with candy and sweets. Like you, they are a type of shifter and can take the appearance of any child they wish, feeding off adults. I fear we may have more than one death on our hands by morning."

"I've already walked the streets of Enchanted Haven and picked up nothing," he informs us.

I fidget, racking my brain for ideas. "They like caves near water. Are there any of those nearby?"

The two exchange a look. "There's the Mortis Caves along the banks of Hangman Gorge," Cyn says.

"A river cuts through the terrain north of here," Torren explains. "High cliffs of limestone and granite."

That sounds like the perfect hideout for them. "Can you fly there and see if you pick up signs of them?"

He screws up his nose. "Fly?"

I wave a hand at his body. "Turn into a bat and take to the skies?"

He laughs again, but this time, the sound is melodic, tripping my heart along with it. "I can do many things, but I'm incapable of turning myself into a winged rodent."

I find I'm somewhat relieved about that. "How far is it to these caves?"

Cyn glances off into the distance. A drizzle has started up. "Three, four miles due west."

On foot, that will take too long. "Do either of you possess a vehicle?"

Cyn starts to reply when a woman's cry rents the night. The hair on the back of my neck stands straight up from the terror-filled sound, and my feet are moving toward her before I can blink.

Chapter Seven

"That came from Main Street," Torren says, keeping pace with me.

Cyn is faster and passes us. I try to skip over a puddle, and the vampyre easily lifts me across it. For the briefest heartbeat, gravity has no hold on me. I'm flying.

My feet hit the pavement once more and I suppress a giggle of glee. The freedom he must experience being able to do that! While he may not transform into a bat and soar, he still possesses incredible abilities.

Another of them is speed. He must hold back for me to keep up with him, the lycan racing ahead to the corner, but he doesn't grow impatient. I'm breathing hard when we reach Main Street, and I pull up short at the sight that greets us.

Cyn has shifted to his werewolf form, and I blink at the silver and black beast snarling at a group of children. They've backed an older woman against the wishing well and are throwing candy at her. She shrieks again, and I race forward.

Torren shouts my name, and Cyn leaps in front of me, blocking my path.

Lifting my skirt, I vault over him. My dexterity shocks even me. Talk about physics! I rush the attackers. "Get away from her!"

These are no ordinary children, and I'm shocked yet another group of Ever After beings is here. These are not kobolds, however.

Torren is beside me before I can blink. He bares his fangs, and they scramble and run away. One of the older children stops and turns back to eye me. "Princess?"

I subtly shake my head. "You have me confused with someone else. Where are your parents?"

He narrows his eyes, and I fear he'll give me away, but instead, the young goblin jets off into the alleyway with the others.

"You could have been hurt," Torren snaps at me.

I'm not used to anyone other than my mother using that tone, and I bridle. "They're goblin-born and meant no harm, only to tease."

"Poor manners are poor manners," the woman says, straightening her jacket. "Just because they get to dress in costume and pretend to be something else does not give them permission to be mean."

Cyn arrives but doesn't shift to his form as the town reverend. The woman is breathing heavily and holding a hand to her chest. "Are you all right?" I ask.

She nods, wary of the enormous wolf watching her. I sense her mind insisting *it's only a dog*. A huge, very hairy beast, but not supernatural in any way. I pet Cyn's head to reinforce that he's harmless to her. "I don't know what has gotten into our youth these days." Candy is scattered at her feet, and she points to it. "That stuff is not only rotting their teeth, it's rotting their brains." Her finger rises to me. "And you shouldn't make up stories to let them off the hook. *Goblins.*" She scoffs. "They could wear angel costumes and still be bullies."

"Dr. Trumble." Torren gestures from her to me. In his gaze, I see a warning. "This is Seraphina Rothschild. She's new to town. Seraphina, this is Maude, our town dentist."

She's mundane. Not only does she not believe in the creatures who attacked her, she doesn't believe in magic.

"Nice to meet you." She pushes off the stone edge, brushing at her pants. She uses her finger to point again. "My clinic is down the block. Be sure to call and set up an appointment. Gets busy this time of year."

"For what?" I ask.

She frowns at me. "For a checkup, of course."

"Oh, I assure you, my teeth are in perfect condition."

The finger wags in my face. "That's what you all say before you come begging me to fill your cavities or yank out your rotten molars."

Torren offers to walk her to her residence above the office. She declines, but I notice how she keeps a watchful eye as she hustles away.

Once she's out of sight, Cyn returns to his human form. "Halloween is always a bit wild here, but this year it seems..."

"What?" Torren asks when Cyn hesitates.

"Freakish, even for us."

Torren turns a fierce gaze on me. "Goblin-born? They weren't kobolds?"

"No. Have a sniff."

Both he and the lycan raise their sensitive noses and inhale. "They smell..."—a crease forms between Torren's brows—"like humans, only earthier."

I do know of goblins who've been exiled from Ever After. They can be a petty, quarrelsome, and generally introverted group. "While they have faults, they are not dangerous."

"It was still reckless of you to chase after them," he insists.

"Why? They will obey me." The two males blink at me as if needing further explanation. *Oops.* I've said too much. "About those caves. Where can we find an automobile?"

Cyn shifts in a flash of light and is instantly a hairy beast again, tall enough to look me in the eyes. "Why use a car when you can take a wolf?" This is said through long canines, slurring his normal speech, but impressive all the same.

"Show off," Torren mutters.

I'm once more puzzled. "You want me to ride you?"

He winks. "Give her a boost, Tor."

The vampyre lifts me before I can protest, and I find myself straddling the giant wolf. "Hang on," Cyn says, and we are off.

I barely maintain my seat, needing to grip chunks of his fur to stay upright as we jet through the night. Torren runs alongside us with an ease I admire, and I notice he's grinning while I fear for my life. The wolf and vampyre seem to be in a race.

A soft drizzle coats us all, and I must continually wipe it from my eyes. This requires me to release one of my hands, which inevitably causes me to tip sideways. More than once, Torren reaches over with fluid grace and gives me a nudge to keep me vertical. "Can you smell them?" I call over the wind rushing past my ears and the growing sound of the river.

"It's getting sharper," Cyn replies, and Torren's grin disappears as he inhales deeply.

We slow, and he says, "There are at least three distinctive beings. Possibly four."

Once you've smelled a kobold, you can't mistake it for anything else. "Is one of them Marlena?"

He keeps his focus on the terrain as we trek over the ground that grows rocky. The landscape is filled with so many trees we must shift this way and that to avoid them. Torren hops left, and we go right around a thick bush, and then he rejoins us. "Afraid not."

I draw a relieved breath. Cyn's black nose drops to the ground as he checks out a section of large boulders. Torren assists me from Cyn's back and leads me to a ledge overlooking the winding river.

"There are plenty of caves along this bluff." He points north, but the clouds are heavy once more. Fog rises from the water. He can see with his vampyre sight far better than I can into the gloom. "It would make sense to use all of them as hiding places, but the largest has tunnels that connect to the others. The problem is, it sits in the lowest section and fills with water at high tide."

It's nearing midnight. "That was hours ago. We should be fine."

Cyn, in human form, joins us. "There is definitely

activity of some kind going on around here. What's our plan?"

"Simple," I say. "Since Marlena is not a prisoner, all we have to do is draw them out and subdue them."

I start walking, and Torren touches my arm, stopping me. "How? They're dangerous creatures."

"*We* are dangerous creatures," I remind him. "Leave it to me. I can and will handle them."

"You?" Cyn chuckles. "No offense, but you're a princess, right? I don't know what kind or from where, but it's obvious. That kid recognized you, and it fits."

"Yes," Torren says. "Explain."

Of all the times for them to put me on the spot. "I can't."

They close in on me, invading my personal space. Both are much taller, and I'm forced to look up to maintain eye contact. The vampyre's voice is low and edged with annoyance. "Why not?"

I stick out a defiant chin. "I can't tell you that either. You'll have to put your suspicions aside for now and trust me. I know these creatures, the goblin children, as well. Not personally, but their kind. My background is not your concern—the kobolds are."

His handsome, perfectly sculpted face becomes lined with a mix of trepidation and annoyance. "Princess or no, the last thing we want is for you to end up dead."

"Yeah," Cyn says. "Look, we all have pasts we're not proud of. Things we wish we'd done differently. Honestly, Seraphina, your secrets are safe with us. I don't care who you are, where you come from, or what you've done. I care about protecting those in my town. Help us with that, and we're cool."

Reluctantly, Torren inclines his head in agreement when Cyn elbows him.

They have no idea what I'm capable of. A ghost floats in the mist and fog, and my breath catches—Izzy. I blink, and she's gone, a figment of my overwhelmed imagination.

I shake off the yawning pit of guilt suddenly stretching out under my feet. *Focus.* "Kobolds seek two things," I tell them. "Blood and sweets. They'll be especially drawn to my—" I stop myself once more before I break my oath never to mention my heritage and bloodline—a near-impossible feat. "I'll handle them. I'm not helpless, and I know what I'm doing."

Cyn scrunches his busy brows together. "But how?"

Torren seems to read my mind. "By using herself as bait."

"No." Cyn rears back. "That's out of the question."

"It certainly is not." Males. Always so protective. Just like Hansel. I sense their need to safeguard and defend me oozing from their pores. "I'm the perfect enticement. You'll see."

Torren glowers. "Why?"

If only I could explain how many creatures are lured by my blood, sweet as spun sugar and filled with magical properties. A kobold would be nearly unstoppable if they were to snack on me. "Isn't it obvious? I'm sweet," I say with a wink, "and have a rare blood type. You, of all creatures, should be able to appreciate that."

"Like AB-negative?" Cyn asks.

Torren is undaunted. Also curious, I garner from the tilt

of his head and the gleam in his eye. "Not that kind of blood," he says. "How rare are you, princess?"

In this world? One of a kind. "The important thing is, I can handle them. I promise. I'll draw them out and make sure they never hurt any in Enchanted Haven again."

The two exchange one of those silent looks filled with thoughts and concerns.

As if coming to an agreement, Torren adjusts the sleeves of his jacket. "We're not using you as bait. We'll handle the confrontation and the capture. You'll remain here and stay out of harm's way."

"Speaking of," Cyn says, "what exactly are we going to do with the critters once we round them up?"

A muscle tics in Torren's jaw. "I'll handle them."

"You two aren't listening to me." Their chauvinism so aggravates me that I want to stomp my foot. That's too much like a spoiled princess, which makes me angry at myself. I set my hands on my hips. "I know kobolds and how to deal with their kind. *I* will trap them and send them back to the realm they came from. The Qu"—I clear my throat—"the *ruler* there will handle their punishment. Believe me, it will be far worse than you can imagine."

Cyn's long hair drifts across his shoulders. "Why are you here instead of there? Did you decide you didn't like it?"

I force a smile. "It's a delightful land, truly, except for a few outliers, such as these creatures." I wish I could paint a picture of Ever After's beauty for them. Dread over the fact I'm no longer welcome there claws at my belly. "I needed to get away. What do you call it? A vacation. Now,"—I march for the caves—"if you'll excuse me, I have kobolds to capture."

Chapter Eight

The pair attempt to dissuade me from my plan, but I ignore their pleas. I've handled more than a few such brutes, and I will not stand for any Ever After monsters to bring more death to this world.

If only I had my chocolate-covered marshmallows to scent the air and gain their attention. Since I don't, I'll have to use my blood.

"We need to watch the entrance, do recon," Torren insists. We crouch a few yards from the entrance of a large, rocky cave. The path is edged with moss; a tree rises from the water nearby, its visible gnarled roots running here and there, white in the moonlight. More trees and bushes grow helter-skelter along the bank and cover the tops of the caverns, towering into the midnight blue sky.

The river smells of fish, but the pungent odor of kobold makes me hold my nose. I must not gag and give us away, but I can only imagine the stench for the vampyre and shifter, whose olfactory abilities are magnified a hundred times over mine. "How can only four beings create this much malodor?"

"They've probably been here a while." He peers through the heavy fog into the mouth of the cave. "By my count, they've murdered at least six humans in the tri-county area, possibly more."

Six! My stomach rolls, even though it's empty. I fight my gag reflex again.

Cyn sighs heavily. "We've been a peaceful community for so long, these attacks have shaken us."

Cradling my nose in the crease of my elbow, I swallow hard, close my eyes, and take a centering breath. "There's no telling how long they've been here. If they stay in one spot for any considerable length of time, law enforcement will catch up with them, but it seems they have grown lazy here. They must have found it to their liking."

This does not sit well with Torren. "Innocent supernaturals may have been wrongly accused, just like my lieutenant. I will see them brought to justice."

His threat is understandable, but I can't allow it. "Releasing the kobolds to human police is a recipe for disaster. They must be returned to our—*their*—realm. I'll do what I can to make sure any innocents who have been wrongly imprisoned are released."

Angered, his eyes glow red as they meet mine. "They will pay for what they've done *here*." He points. "If we can't turn them over to the police, then I will take care of them tonight."

My magic is swirling inside me, and my own anger is rising. "Absolutely not. I appreciate your point of view, but causing their deaths and having their blood on your hands is as dangerous for you as turning them over is. They may appear children, but don't let that fool you. They are dangerous creatures like none you've encountered previously." This isn't helping my case for taking them on myself, but I must warn him. "If I haven't made it clear, they are *not of this world*, and no one in it can contain them. They are near immortal, and unleashing your desire for vengeance on them will only cause you and your town more problems. I thought you wanted to protect those who live here; if you attack the kobolds, they will destroy this place."

Cyn shakes his head, picking at a layer of moss on a rock. "I don't like it either, but we should do what she says, Tor. She knows them. We don't."

The vampyre looks away, seething, but returns his gaze to mine within seconds. His eyes no longer glow red. "For now, we'll follow your lead, but if this goes poorly for us, I will do what needs to be done."

Still peeved, I bite my inner cheek before I respond. "I appreciate your confidence in me."

It's said with too much sarcasm, but he doesn't comment further. His energy, however, says it all. He believes I'll fail, and he is on a knife's edge, ready to slaughter those inside.

I bump my shoulder into his, attempting to ease his intensity. "While I can't resurrect the dead"—although I wish I could—"to bring back your friend, I will free the innocent. Again, I ask for you to have faith in me."

The tenseness in his face softens. The brutal, vicious energy swirling around him does as well. "Whatever I can do to assist, please tell me."

I hold out my wrist. "Bite me."

A brow lifts under a lock of hair that's fallen across his forehead. "Excuse me?"

"Draw my blood. It will bring them running, remember?"

It's apparent that he prefers to think things through and to be as prepared as one can. "Wouldn't it be wiser to take them by surprise?"

If things were different, I'd agree with such a strategy. "Time is of the essence. You and Cyn will be the surprise." I smile brightly, keeping my true intent secret. I'm the only one who can deal with the kobolds. The best I can hope for is to keep the vampyre and werewolf out of their clutches. "Now, bite my wrist, and the two of you hide in the bushes. When our quarry appears, I'll offer them a treat they can't resist. Once they're under my spell, you will subdue them and keep watch while I call..." I catch myself again. "The proper authorities from their world."

Perhaps the Queen will see this as my attempt to get back in her good graces. Maybe I should look at it that way myself.

I don't. While my arrival in this realm hasn't gone smoothly, I have a taste of freedom here that I've never enjoyed in my homeland. I can make a difference here. Help people—both supernatural *and* human.

Torren takes my hand, raising my wrist toward his mouth. He hesitates, his gaze meeting mine over the pale expanse of my skin. The blue veins pulse in time with my heartbeat. "You're sure?"

My heart twists in my chest, leaping at the smoldering look in his eyes. The sharing of blood means a great deal to him. While it is, in this instance, a means to an end, he does not take it lightly.

It's my turn to hesitate. My voice comes out breathy, vulnerable. "Does this constitute a bargain I'm unaware of?"

The corner of his mouth twitches. "You could always let Cyn do it."

I don't want him. I want Torren. I clear my throat and refocus my intentions, refusing to let that predatory gaze unhinge me. "You'll be sufficient, but so we are clear, nothing about this deed holds either of us in debt to the other. Agreed?"

A grin breaks free. "Agreed."

As he's about to sink his fangs into my tender skin, Marlena lands in front of us, the tip of her blade pointed at his throat. "Do it, and I'll dump your Undead body in the river behind you."

Chapter Nine

"Marlena!" I abandon Torren to throw my arms around her neck. "Where have you been?"

"Scouting." She glares at my companions. "The three little pigs. What are you doing here?"

"Not a pig," Cyn says grumpily. "The Three Musketeers, on the other hand..." He bows. "At your service."

Marlena holds back an eye roll. She draws me aside. "What are you thinking? If that vampyre had bitten you, all manner of problems would now be in your lap."

"He was only doing as I instructed. I must draw out the kobolds hiding in that cave to dispatch them back to the realm."

She tips the end of her sword toward the fog-encased opening. "The cave is deserted. I tracked them to a spot a few miles downriver, but the trail disappeared. They used the water to cover it and conceal themselves."

My shoulders slump. "They realized we would come for them."

She lowers the sword, slipping it into its sheath. "We need to regroup and come at this fresh tomorrow. In the light of day, we may be able to pick up a physical trail. They won't return here."

She's correct, and I'm deflated, knowing I've failed. My failure could bring death to more innocents. "They'll move to another town and pick their next victim."

With a gentle hand, she steers me toward the males. "Return her to the jailhouse. I'll find a place to spend the night."

I jerk away. "I can't go back there."

Torren nods at my godmother. "I'll make sure she is safe."

Marlena snorts. "Right. I'd rather the lycan took that role."

Torren sighs. "I assure you, I would never harm her."

"I'm afraid I can't sneak her back inside City Hall," Cyn tells her. "Torren's the only one who can do that."

Her lips press together in a hard line, and she regards me with a touch too much disappointment but finally relents. "Fine, but my threat stands."

Torren takes my hand. "I give my word."

"I never expected to hand you over to a vampyre for safe-keeping," she says under her breath.

Cyn hears the comment and attempts to assure her. "Seraphina will be taken care of, and you can bed down in my rectory if you like. No one will disturb you there."

Withdrawing my hand from Torren's, I sniff. "I'll be staying there as well." I start walking, unconcerned if they accompany me. Life at court has taught me that if I act confident, others will follow my lead, even if they may not want to. "I'll deal with Mayor Jo tomorrow." The pause behind me suggests none of them likes being ignored, nor do they like my idea. I like it very much. "We can brainstorm ideas on how to track down the kobolds and round them up. The goblin children may have insight."

A heartbeat of hesitation and then footsteps sound from behind me. Smiling, I continue along the path, taking in the landscape. I mentally note the types of trees, plants, and bushes we pass. There are a few unknowns; I'll need to research them once this is over. My feet brush against trailing mint vines, releasing their sweet scent. I reach down and collect several sprigs, lifting them to my nose. I'll add them to a cup of tea in the morning, saving one to propagate for future candies.

Marlena catches up to me, and I wave the springs under her nose. "There is an apothecary of healing plants and trees here," I tell her. "Along with sweets, perhaps we should offer potions and tinctures."

"Perhaps."

She is still angry. I consider how to smooth things over. "Humans and supernaturals in Enchanted Haven could benefit from your skills, you know."

She was once an accomplished healer, along with being a soldier. "One step at a time, princess. We haven't landed the building yet."

The males cannot walk side-by-side with us on the narrow trail. Torren scouts ahead, and Cyn brings up the rear. "Tell the mayor everything you told us," he says to me, "and he'll be more than happy to extend credit for the building."

Torren glances back. "If he refuses, there are other

options. I own several rental properties, and I'm willing to loan you one."

A building is a big responsibility, and we must also secure lodging. In my mind, the costs add up. In Ever After, I never worried about currency. The exchange of goods and services is different there. Here, humans are consumed with making money and spending it. Everything has a cost. "I've seen pictures of those traveling venues. Food trucks. One of those would be nice." *And cheaper*.

"All of us working together will figure out an acceptable plan," Tor says.

"Oh, goodie," Marlena grumbles.

The return to town is much slower than riding on the wolf's back, but I use the time to consider two courses of action—one for capturing the kobolds, the other for starting my new sweet shop. Only a few hours ago, I thought my life was over. Surrounded by the three of them, purpose burning in my veins, I sense I have dodged my unfortunate circumstances.

If only Izzy could see me now.

I raise my eyes to the stars overhead and make another wish. I imagine she is walking with us, singing a cheerful tune, replying to the owl hooting in the distance, and calling to any forest faeries watching us pass by from hidden places between tree roots and under rocks. I ask what she thinks about me opening a sweet shop and imagine her nodding and making a list of candies and other products I should carry. It's almost as if I can feel her nudging me as she watches Torren's handsome figure ahead, encouraging me to flirt with him.

As if he senses my gaze, he peeks over his shoulder and

offers a grin. Marlena pulls me close, scowling, but I can't suppress the grin I return. He is wickedly delicious, and I sense he will never hurt me, yet I am once more afraid my gullibility may be why I believe such a thing.

My plan to delay speaking to Mayor Jo tomorrow is thwarted when we arrive at the chapel and find him waiting for us. "I thought you were in jail," he says, giving Torren and Cyn a chastising look.

Marlena hugs my waist. "We're spending the night here discussing ways to handle your homicide problem. Perhaps you'd like to join us."

If her defensive and commanding tone takes him aback, he doesn't show it. He lifts his chin towards Cyn. "Do you still have that bottle of Irish whiskey handy? I could use a drink."

"There are no small glasses in my house." The werewolf winks. "So let's enjoy it."

Marlena releases me as they climb the stairs. Torren gestures for me to stay back. As they enter the double doors, he lowers his voice. "Am I welcome to stay? I know you don't need my protection, but I would offer it anyway."

"Of course. We must discuss the kobold issue, and I assume you're helping with that."

"Your godmother does not like me."

"Then I suppose you need to win her over."

We share a smile again, and he escorts me up the steps.

In Ever After, we honor nature and the seasons. We believe there is a soul in every living thing, and we respect that. I have never entered a human place of worship before and am speechless as I take in the church's beauty. Towering ceilings, arched glass windows, intricate candelabras, and beautiful paintings of serene saints. The architecture alone is astounding, the interior decorating lush compared to the plain exterior. I would have never guessed the building held such intricate archways and columns.

We pass through a central room with pews adorned in red velvet upholstery. They look surprisingly comfortable, and I reach out to run my hand over the soft material. It's gloriously soft. A raised platform with a giant mahogany table, as well as a pulpit, anchors one end. A piano, organ, and harp rest at the outer edges, and rows of chairs look out over the expansive nave.

Cyn opens a nearly invisible door on one side and motions us through. Mayor Jo and Marlena converse quietly as Cyn leads us all to a kitchen.

Compared to the previous room, this is smaller but not cramped with all five of us in it. I opt for tea, plunking a few mint leaves in the brewing liquid, while the others, except Torren, help themselves to the liquor. I notice how both the mayor and my godmother look...happy.

She explains about the kobolds. Torren confesses how he broke me out of jail. Mayor Jo is annoyed about it yet is swayed to think I'm innocent. Cyn lends insight into tracking our quarry, and Marlena assures him they will be dealt with by the leaders of our 'country.' He doesn't argue, seeming almost relieved that she'll handle it.

Several times during all these discussions, I want to jump in and add my thoughts and suggestions, but I keep them to myself, studying the group dynamics instead. Could this be my new family?

"You have to return to the jail," Mayor Jo tells me, raising a hand to fend off my argument. "Not because I don't believe you're innocent, but the guards and other mundanes will see your escape as an omission of guilt. Torren will be questioned and could end up behind bars with you. We do this the right way—I'll produce new evidence in the case, clearing you as a suspect. You'll be officially released by noon tomorrow, I promise. Otherwise, you'll be considered on the run, and that will cause you more trouble."

"We don't want that," Marlena says more to me than him. "How do we sneak her back in?"

The idea of returning to the cell makes my skin crawl, but I understand he's following the rules of this land. My gaze tracks to the vampyre next to me, the way his fingers tease along the side of my arm. I don't wish him to be incarcerated with me, and yet, the idea has its appeal.

Torren sits forward. "The same I got her out. Don't worry. No one will suspect a thing."

Cyn looks doubtful but not over Torren's plan. "How will you fabricate evidence that clears her name, Mayor?"

"Let me worry about that," he says. "Finish your tea, Seraphina, and then let Torren return you to my precinct."

We are quiet as he leaves, Marlena's eyes tracking him until he disappears. I linger over my drink, my mind and emotions raw.

* * *

Inside the dreary cell, I wake at sunrise, the first bars of light shooting through a high window at the far end of the row of cells. I've slept little and am sore from the uncomfortable bench. The ghost is back, smiling and humming as she perches on the end of the cot. "There you are," Flower says as if we're old friends. "I thought you'd never get up."

I wonder if she will follow me when I'm released. I also wonder if Torren is waiting outside like he promised to be. My dress is wrinkled, and I try to smooth it out, my hair tangled in knots. "How far from these walls can you go?"

She tips her head up, tapping a finger against her chin in thought. "Not sure. I saw what you did last night to save the dentist. That was nice of you."

"I'm sorry you're stuck here."

Her eyes turned to me. "Why?"

"You can't possibly enjoy hanging around this place."

She stands and hovers, scanning the room. "It's not so bad. I hear a lot of gossip here. Say, do you have any of that sparkly stuff from last night?"

"What type of gossip?"

She peeks under the cot. "The whos, the hows, the whys. You know, all the stuff about suspects and cases. It's like my personal true crime show." Not finding the faery dust, her face becomes forlorn. "For instance, I know you're getting released in a few minutes. They found evidence pointing to the real killer." Her eyes widen as she emphasizes the last three words. She lowers her voice to a whisper. "You'll never believe who it is."

I sit up straighter. "Who?"

She glances around as if searching for eavesdroppers, then floats closer, putting her face in front of mine. "You better be careful."

"Why? Who is it?"

"The killer is..." She grins as if teasing me with the juicy tidbit.

"Please, Flower, tell me."

"If I do, will you get me more of that dust?"

She's already hooked on it, but it's not meant for humans. It could lead to a drug addiction far worse than anything they have access to. But she's a ghost. Would it affect her the same? There's no time to figure it out. "Yes, yes," I agree.

Again, her voice comes out a whisper, and there's a manic gleam in her eye. "You'll never believe it." She is giddy with the news. "It's a vampyre."

Chapter Ten

Mayor Jo releases me from the cell, leading me to his office and closing the door behind us. "There's something I'd like you to see."

I hesitate. "I don't feel comfortable about you accusing an innocent vampyre of this deed. You know it's a kobold."

"Sure about that?" He points to a screen on his desk and clicks a button.

A grainy image appears, and I suck in a breath. A man carries the lifeless body of our victim, laying him in the spot where he was discovered during the party. The coat, the dark, perfectly coifed hair, the set of his shoulders...it's all far too familiar.

Torren. I swallow the sick feeling pushing its way up my throat. "Does he show his face?"

"Does he need to? What time did you say you arrived here?"

I think back to the gas station. The news had played

softly in the background next to a large wall clock. "I believe it was around seven thirty-ish."

He points to a timestamp in the lower right corner. "This took place less than twenty-nine minutes later. So Torren could have witnessed your confrontation with Luca Hudson, killed him while you were inside, and deposited his body behind town hall before returning to escort you to the party."

My head swims. "For what reason would he kill this man and frame me for it?"

"I don't know, but I plan to find out."

I collapse into a brown wooden chair, a hand gripping the armrest. "That makes no sense. Torren didn't even know me at that point." And still doesn't.

"You were an easy scapegoat. But now, he likes you, or is pretending to. I want you to stick close to him and see if you can get hard evidence tying him to Hudson's murder."

My insides threaten a revolt, and I cross both arms over my lower half. "You can't be serious."

He points to the recording. "Without seeing his face, this proves nothing. He'll put up his guard if I bring him in for questioning. At the moment, you and I are the only ones who know about this, and that's how we're going to keep it."

Flower drifts in. "Well, I know."

He doesn't acknowledge her, and I wonder why a divine being such as himself can't see or hear the dead. "Killers often insert themselves into a case to keep tabs on it," he continues. "He may have been so friendly last night because he was setting you up all along."

I swallow past the lump in my throat. "I know it was the kobold."

"Then find me evidence of that. If it was, why was Torren carrying that body and dumping it behind City Hall for us to find?"

I have no plausible reason. Torren told the mayor I smelled of Hudson's blood, landing me in that cell. Regardless of that, he aided my escape. Could Mayor Jo be correct, and he's only pretending to like me? I must be careful with all this. I've known these people for less than a day and am unfamiliar with how this dimension works.

I scrutinize the mayor's face for any hint of mistruth or manipulation. I see none, but that doesn't mean he's not trying to work an angle because he holds a secret grudge against the vampyre. On the other hand, if Torren is guilty and is trying to frame me, I am more than motivated to turn the tables on him. "What kind of evidence do you need?"

Mayor Jo reels off a list of options and I listen carefully. When he finishes, he asks, "Got it?"

"And what will you do for me?"

My question surprises him. "I've already offered you a deal on the empty candy shop."

I doubt he's ever bargained with someone like me. "If I'm able to prove who this killer is, I expect more than that."

"Such as?"

I stand, regaining my composure. "I'll get back to you about it. Now, will you show me the building? I want to make sure it will fit my needs."

Marlena waits outside on a bench and jumps up as we exit. She seems to be in high spirits, but I suspect it's because of the mayor as much as I'm free.

The air is crisp and cool, whirlwinds of leaves rattling on the sidewalk as we make our way down the block. The exterior of the two-story structure is brick. Mayor Joe retrieves a ring of keys from his front pocket, a skeleton one sliding into the door's brass lock.

Sunlight streams from the large display windows, illuminating the high ceilings and the golden wooden floors. Here and there, light scratches mark the wood. The walls are pale yellow with tiny blue forget-me-nots painted in a cheerful frame around the doors and windows. Black-and-white photographs of the town are the only other decor, giving the room an almost forgotten feeling. The place is steeped in the faint smell of must, and dust moats float in the sunbeams.

In my mind, I re-imagine it. The once-bustling shop is filled with the sounds of phones ringing, the smell of baking cookies, and patrons chatting while they enjoy tasty treats. Glass jars hold pretty candies, and children stare in fascination at varieties of their favorites. From the corner of my eyes, I catch echoes of the past, the translucent ghosts coming and going as if they are still here.

There is a hefty counter with a vintage brass register. My fingers trail over the old numbered knobs, and again, I feel the past coming to life around me.

I force my mind from it to consider the future. Shelves line a wall, and a lovely display case is part of the counter. In the windows, I can show off plates of confectioneries, brownies, and cookies to lure customers inside.

Marlena, ever the practical one, calls to me from the rear room. "The kitchen needs an overhaul, but you must see the skylight and bay window."

Sure enough, the empty room has lovely natural lighting

and plenty of space for setting up my equipment and supplies. I move toward the window, delighted to see a garden of wildflowers in the tidy backyard. The space is small but lovely, and I am already making plans for the herbs I can grow there.

"Does this still work?" Marlena asks Mayor Jo, checking out the generous fireplace in the corner.

It has a grand mantlepiece adorned with intricate carvings. "Sure does," he tells her.

My fingers once more journey over this piece of the past, and I wonder what the images symbolize. I can hardly wait to research them, the skin of my hand tingling from the magic it's infused with. "Was the previous store owner a supernatural?" I ask.

"As mundane as they come." He points across the way. "The fridge still works, too."

That also appears to be a remnant from days gone by, along with the oven next to it. The door is rusty, and I'm afraid to open it for fear it may fall off. Under my feet, the hardwood has been covered by black and white checkered tiles. I tap a foot against it, estimating it will take hours to clean off the layers of grime that have collected over the years.

It's far from perfect, but with some elbow grease and magic, it will be all mine.

Marlena steps close as I stare into the backyard. Most of the flowers have gone dormant in the cool weather, but some still bloom with beautiful abandon. "What do you think?" she asks.

"Don't forget," Mayor Joe says, "there's a furnished apartment upstairs."

My godmother and I exchange a look. Based on the

downstairs, it could be hideous, but considering our circumstances, it's better than nothing.

As one, we turn to him. "We'll take it," I say.

He claps his hands together. "I'll have my assistant, Betty, draw up the contract."

I walk him to the door, and he hands me the skeleton key. "Just remember our deal," I remind him.

He nods solemnly. "Of course. Don't forget about the turnovers." He winks and takes off down the sidewalk back to City Hall.

"What was that about?" Marlena asks. "What kind of deal?"

"I had him pegged as an angel food cake guy, but he prefers turnovers." I shrug, hoping she doesn't press the matter. "My magic must still be wonky. Now, which project do we tackle first?"

She senses there's more to it but doesn't grill me. Her gaze lands on a framed picture. "I swear that couple was standing on the other side of that building when we entered."

We both move in, scrutinizing the photograph. I've barely glanced at any of them, too busy sizing up the space and thinking about how to remodel it. They're dressed in attire from the Victorian age, expressions somber. The building appears to be this one. "I bet those were the original owners. Since then, the place next door was built, and the siding was replaced with brick, but I'm sure that's here."

The lace curtain seems to move in the second-floor window, and we both rear back, startled.

"What was that?" she asks.

Glancing at the ceiling as if I could see through to the

apartment above us, I have a feeling we'll find out, like it or not. "What are the odds we have a resident ghost?"

She shivers visibly. "Don't even kid about that. You know how I feel about the dead."

"We have to check the upstairs."

She draws her sword. "I'm not living here if it's haunted."

I hide my smile as I head to the staircase that leads to the apartment. "I'm sure Cyn would let you continue to sleep in the church."

She makes a noise in the back of her throat, suggesting she is neither humored by that nor reassured. "I can't decide if I like this town or not. Vampyres, lycans, ghosts..."

"Not to mention goblins and kobolds."

"Goblins?"

"Afraid so. I'm sure they're children of Outcasts."

The steps creak under our feet as we ascend. A few hours ago, I was sure this was the perfect town for us. With my doubts about Torren sitting like a lump in my chest and my failed efforts to locate the kobolds and send them back to Ever After, I fear I have stumbled into a story with no happy ending.

Chapter Eleven

The apartment has three rooms plus a bath. Peeling wallpaper in the central area reveals a layer of uneven plaster under it, and well-worn furniture, covered in what appears to be cat hair, is scattered haphazardly around.

Cobwebs hang from corners, silky strands catching the sunlight filtering through the narrow, arched windows. The kitchen is barely big enough for my godmother and me to be in simultaneously but appears functional with the same setup as downstairs. The refrigerator and stove are more modern than the furniture but still decades outdated.

Large cedar wardrobes in each bedroom are filled with clothes that smell like the former owners. One holds men's trousers and ladies' dresses, the other children's attire.

No ghosts appear, and for that, I'm grateful, but the child's bedroom is the coldest place on this floor.

Back in the central area, I feel my chest tighten. A family portrait sits on an upright piano against the far wall, the top coated in a thick layer of dust. "I wonder how long this place has been empty. Surely someone lived here after the original family moved." *Or died*, I refrain from saying.

Marlena closes her eyes and then smiles when she reopens them. "How about we get breakfast, then decide where to start with renovations?"

"We have our work cut out for us, don't we?"

"I knew it wouldn't be easy, but yes, we do."

A giggle causes me to pivot in the direction of the second bedroom. I see nothing and notice that Marlena doesn't seem to hear it. Am I genuinely hallucinating this time? Or is the child's spirit teasing me?

My confidence of the previous day evaporates as quickly as the playful laughter. "It's so different here. One minute, I feel right at home," I tell her. "The next, I feel like a fish out of water."

She places a hand on her sword hilt and puts an arm around my shoulders, drawing me toward the exit. "You'll feel better with food in your stomach."

I descend ahead of her, but I am unsure of what to do on the first floor. "Humans use currency we don't have to purchase things." In Ever After, we mostly barter and trade. "We have none of that. We can't buy a meal or the ingredients to make it."

She offers a wink. "Cyn invited us for breakfast. The only catch is—he claims he can't cook."

The thought of food is a balm to my heart. She's right—once I've eaten, I'll be ready to tackle everything I need to do.

Everything except confronting Torren.

I push that thought out of my mind. It will be good to use my hands and work on the shop while I come up with ideas on how to prove his innocence—or guilt. I consider creating a candy that would force him to tell me the truth, although I'll only do that as a last resort. Using such means on someone I still consider a friend is not something I take lightly. It will break the bond of trust beyond repair.

The church kitchen appears larger today, with its countertops and a commercial stove gleaming. Marlena sets a table on the other side of the pass-through between the main cooking area and a dining space. There are six round tables with chairs, each covered by a distinctive and colorful fall cloth. A coffee maker percolates, and the scent mixes with that of butter, vanilla, and cinnamon. I hum as I flip the pancakes and listen to Cyn tell us about the town and its inhabitants.

When we take our seats to dive in, I cover my stack with maple syrup. The three of us eat in silence for several minutes, enjoying ourselves. When we are nearly finished, I sip coffee and toy with the remnants of my breakfast. "How long have you known Torren?"

By the gleam in his eye, he thinks I'm asking because I am romantically attracted to the vampyre. I wish to go back to last night when that seemed possible. "He and his nest have been here longer than I have, but I've always found him to be the most levelheaded of the supernaturals around here. His group keeps to themselves, and I know he is sometimes at odds with the upper-level vamps in the region because of his rules. In general, shifters and the Undead don't get along, but he's reasonable and seeks to keep the peace between all of us."

"How does he feel about humans?"

"Like I said, he keeps his nest away from trouble."

Was that true? "He told me about one of the recent

attacks. He thought his lieutenant was responsible, and he had to dole out the punishment."

Cyn mops up the relics of syrup with a morsel of pancake. "I almost didn't move to Enchanted Haven because of the vampyres, but I've never regretted the decision, and it's because of him. He keeps his word, and he's done a lot for the town to keep it safe from outsiders. There are always those who would start a war between us and the humans or encourage fighting amongst ourselves." He offers me a sincere smile. "You have nothing to fear from him. He's been alone the whole time I've known him, and I think you would be good for him. Get him out of his shell more. He's so busy taking care of his nest he's forgotten what it's like to have fun."

Marlena regards me closely. Her intense stare makes my skin prickle.

"I have too much to worry about to contemplate a romance." I keep my eyes averted from both, pretending to be preoccupied with finishing my food. "I simply want to get to know my neighbors."

The shifter kicks back in his chair, stretching his long legs over to the side and downing the last of his coffee. "I'm an open book. Ask me anything."

To make good on my statement, I pepper him with a few questions about his past. He talks about his calling to help the supernatural world with their spirituality and speaks passionately about his church. When I ask how many parishioners he has, his enthusiasm quells. "Three, but I'm working on it. Torren is helping me with a marketing plan to get the word out."

Marlena tosses her napkin on her empty plate and rubs

her belly. "That was delicious. Thank you. I'd love to stay and find out about the mayor, but we have a lot of work to do. The shop and apartment won't clean themselves."

"I'll make you a deal." He stands and begins to stack our plates. "You help me wash these up, and I'll spend the rest of the day assisting you."

It's a deal we cannot pass up, but Marlena winks at me when I roll up my sleeves to run water in the sink. "I've got this."

With a snap of her fingers, the plates lift one by one to shower themselves under the running water. A scrub brush joins in, removing the sticky residue of the syrup, and each plate rinses itself, landing in the dish drainer.

Our new friend stands back, mouth open as he watches. The cups are next, and finally, the pan. We're done in under three minutes and walking out of the church. Cyn carries buckets, a mop, and a few scrub brushes. "That was..." He glances at my godmother. "Can you do that with *everything*?"

"Only if I want to end up sick as a gorgebubby."

"Sorry, what?"

"Um...?" She glances at me with a *help* look on her face.

"A rabbit who eats until it's so fat, it falls sick," I explain. "A rare creature where we come from."

She snaps her fingers. "What is it you say? Sick as a dog?" She bites her lip, realizing that might not have been the best phrase, but Cyn shows no annoyance. "Using magic always has a price. Even for those of us who have it coursing through our veins. A little sprinkled here and there doesn't harm us, but if we use large doses of it or use it continually, we can end up with a variety of illnesses."

Entering the shop, I pause, listening to the tiny bell above the door jingle. Is it odd that I feel like I'm returning home? Even though the musty smell and dust welcome us, I transport my imagination into the future again and visualize what a wonderful place it will be.

Under the downstairs kitchen sink, we discover cleaning products and rags. We go to work, Marlena cleaning the large windows, Cyn scrubbing the floors, and I tackle the kitchen. A few hours in, I'm bent over, scouring the stains from inside the oven and lost in thought about the last stove I was near. Renewed guilt over Izzy wells up inside me, and I dash away a tear that slips from my eye. I feel cool air sliding over my skin and turn to find Torren inside the rear door, watching me. I straighten, wiping my forehead with the back of my hand, and ignore my racing heart. "I'm sorry. Did I miss your knock, or do you normally enter someone's home without permission?"

His eyes cloud at my curt tone. "Mayor Jo said you were here and suggested I offer my services."

This is my chance to convince him I'm a friend worth confiding in. Plus, the more help, the better. I motion at the oven door, hanging at a useless angle. "Are you any good at fixing appliances?"

He eyes the broken hinge. "Why not replace it?"

"I have no money to do so, and I can't bake the turnovers the mayor has requested without a properly working oven."

He removes his jacket and hangs it on a peg near the door. "Do you have a toolbox?"

"No."

He checks several drawers, discovering a few random

screws and a screwdriver, then motions me away. "Allow me."

A few nimble attempts, and he fixes it, no magic needed. It squeaks when he tests it, but I can't hide my delight. "It will do for now. Thank you."

A snap of his fingers and the teeth-gritting noise stops. "What's next?"

So much for no magic.

All of us work until dusk. We're dirty and tired but satisfied with a job well done. "How about I pick up some food from Trudy's?" Cyn asks. "We can spread a blanket on the floor up front and have a picnic for dinner."

My stomach growls. "What is Trudy's?"

"The diner down the street," Torren says.

I wonder again if he eats regular food. "Do they have anything on the menu that you like?"

He gives a rueful smile. "She has a special plate just for vampyres."

I'm certain I don't want to know what's included in *that* meal. "You've been so kind today," I tell Cyn. "I hate to impose on you even more."

He's halfway out the door, waving me off. "I'll bring back a variety."

"Is there a place where we can wash the bed linens?" Marlena points upstairs. "If I have to sleep here, I'm sleeping on clean sheets."

Torren washes his hands, scrubbing at some grease under his nails. "The church has a washer and dryer. I'm sure Cyn wouldn't mind if you use them."

She nods and takes off upstairs, leaving Torren and me alone. He must sense my trepidation at this, and he steps back, drying his hands, to create space between us. "Have I upset you somehow? Offended you?"

I try not to see the recording of the man with Hudson's body behind City Hall. Try not to feel my heart sink all over again at Mayor Jo's suggestion that Torren is only pretending to like me. "It's been a long day, that's all."

He grabs a stack of clean plates and cups while I fiddle with silverware from a drawer. There are only a few cafe tables, none of which are big enough for all of us to sit at, so we slide them over to a wall to create a spot for our picnic.

Marlena returns, a bundle of sheets and blankets in her arms. "Grab one of the church's tablecloths and bring it back," I tell her.

The vampyre and I are truly alone when she leaves. I offer a vague excuse about wanting to inspect the garden outback. He follows me, a purple twilight wrapping around us as I wander along the tangled overgrowth, wildflowers, and trees. I feel the natural magic and see lights dancing in my peripheral vision. Faeries? Something else?

"It's peaceful here," he says.

I stare into the faces of several cheery pansies. "It is."

"My trackers have not been able to pick up the scent of the kobolds. I thought you would want to know."

Another task on my list. At least he has initiated this conversation. "Did you know the man who was killed?"

"I did not."

I move onto a row of lavender plants. Wild thyme creeps beneath their branches. "I wonder if anyone here did. Perhaps he was a tourist?"

"Does it matter?"

"I'm curious. I plan to return to the river to investigate

where our killers were living, but I'd like to know more about the victim and why he was targeted."

It must sound reasonable to him. "What if we question the gas station attendant? The police interviewed her, but she might have remembered something in the meantime and be more receptive to speaking to you. Not everyone is comfortable with law enforcement, and I've been known to put people at ease."

With his vampyre skills? Either way, I can discuss the case further with him. "A brilliant idea. After dinner?"

He nods, seeming relieved. He holds a hand over a dying rose, and it perks up, its fading beauty restored. "I'm glad you're here."

"Yes," I say, amazed at his magic. I so long for us to be friends. For him to be innocent. "Me, too."

I only hope my recent wishes come true, and I don't regret throwing myself in league with him *or* the mayor.

Chapter Twelve

After a delightful picnic dinner on the shop's floor, we all visit the gas station. The same attendant is on duty but claims she doesn't remember Luca Hudson from any visits before he accosted me. While she falls easily under the spell of the vampyre, even without his use of compulsion, she eyes Marlena and me with guarded speculation.

Cyn purchases a bag of chips and four bottles of a sweet drink, which seems to appease her. She doesn't ask about the magical disappearance she witnessed, nor does she call the police, which relieves my anxiety.

Over the next week, I make no progress in tracking down evidence on either Torren or the kobolds. He shows up daily to help with the building maintenance, as does Cyn. Mayor Jo also stops by, his keen eyes secretly asking if I've secured the proof he's demanded, and each time, I must shake my head.

The kobolds are still missing, and Marlena, Cyn, Torren,

and I institute a nightly patrol to search in case they return. This gives me plenty of opportunities to get to know the vampyre better, yet does nothing to advance either of my causes.

Mayor Jo shares details about Hudson and I manage to catch Flower floating outside City Hall. She's forgotten about the faery dust, thankfully. "Did you see the murder?" I query her. "Or the person who placed the body behind this building?"

Her eyes grow round behind her thick glasses. "There was a murder?"

"That's why I was in jail, remember? I was the suspect? You saw Mayor Jo's video recording and told me about it."

Her lips form an 'O.' "That's right. There *was* a murder. That's kind of scary, isn't it?"

"Do you know who committed it?"

"What was I doing that night?" She taps a finger to her temple. "I can't remember..." I suspect she doesn't remember much, period. "Wait..."

My hopes rise as she scrunches up her face. They're dashed a second later when she blinks and grins. "You had that sparkly stuff that tasted so sweet. What was it? Some type of sugar. Can I get more of that?"

I sigh. "Yes, but I need help with something in return."

"Sure." She nods enthusiastically. "Anything."

"I need you to coax a young boy's spirit to move on and stop haunting my new candy shop."

"There's another ghost in town?"

I refrain from sighing audibly again. "There are several, in fact. I'm not sure what happened to this child, but I can't imagine he enjoys being stuck in my house."

"You moved into a haunted house?"

This is getting me nowhere. "I'm leasing the former bakery on Main Street. There's an apartment upstairs. The original owners are long gone, but their son hangs around." Several times in the past few days, he's left toys in the middle of the floor, and I've heard him giggling again. "Can you talk to him? Encourage him to move onto the afterlife?"

"I suppose. What should I say?"

Best to start with something easy. "Can you offer to be his friend?"

"I'm not really into kids."

"Never mind." It was worth a try, but it's time to abandon this sinking ship. "If you hear anything about Luca Hudson or remember seeing who left his body behind City Hall, let me know."

"Luca? He's dead?" Her hand flies to her heart. "Why didn't you tell me?"

Was she this scatterbrained while among the living? I sure hope the faery dust didn't cause this forgetfulness. "Did you know him?"

"He was a troublemaker. I mean, I didn't wish him dead, but..."

"But what?"

"He was a thief, and he was caring for his brother's son —or so he claimed. That kid was..." She shivers. "Luca stole from my friend, Naria, and that nephew of his gave me the creeps."

No doubt, because the child was actually a kobold. "What did Luca steal from your friend?"

"I tried to warn her about him, but no, she wouldn't listen. Said she could take care of herself." She leans in and lowers her voice. "She's a vampyre, you know. A tough character, to be sure, until he stole her grandmother's necklace. Claimed he was innocent when she confronted him, but she knew he'd done it."

"Naria is a vampyre?"

A nod. "I tried it—blood." She grimaces. "Not my cup of tea. Or coffee. Or anything."

"Is Naria part of Torren's nest?"

"He's cute, right? Very rogue of him to break you out of jail the other night." She winks.

Her memory seems fine about *that* fact. "Yes, quite. You know him, then, because of your friend?"

"Nah. Not really. He's a king or something, but he's kind of a loner. Never partied with us. Naria had the biggest crush on him."

Maybe I'm finally getting somewhere. "Did she tell him about Luca and the necklace?"

A lone butterfly, lost on his migration path, catches her attention. She watches it flutter past into a bush. "What?"

I repeat the question, thinking she is as childlike as those she claims not to be "into."

"Oh, uh. I don't think so. Naria thought she would handle it on her own."

Was it possible she'd kill the thief to retrieve the necklace? My pulse picks up speed. "Do you think she did? Handle it, I mean?"

A shrug. Her finger slips toward the butterfly as if she might encourage it to land on her. "Must have. She was wearing it the night of the party."

"She was at City Hall?"

"Yep." The insect flies about, passing right through her outstretched arm. She laughs. "That tickles."

"Where can I find your friend?"

She blinks at me and seems startled, as if she's forgotten we've been talking. "Who?"

I press my lips together so I don't swear. "Naria. How can I find her?"

"Oh, she's around. She hangs out most nights at the club in Baldwell."

"Is it a vampyre club?"

"That's where I tried blood once. Did I tell you?"

Realizing she's once more of little use, I beg off and find Mayor Jo, detailing what she's confessed to knowing about Luca. He stares at me with a mix of concern and astonishment. "You speak to ghosts?"

Whoops. "Don't you see what this means? Naria had a motive to kill Luca, and she's a vampyre."

"So you no longer believe a kobold murdered Luca?"

"I'm not ruling it out, but this is a lead you need to pursue."

"*Me*?" His angelic energy trembles. "You think I should waltz into a vampyre club and ask questions about a homicide that mimics a vampyre attack?"

"Yes." I'm confused as to why he's opposed to doing so. "Why not?"

He frowns. "Oh, I don't know. Possibly because they might kill me?"

I doubt that, and I do my best to encourage him to find a way, but I'm the one who is offered the opportunity on a plate later that evening.

When I return to the shop, Marlena is finishing up a blackberry pie. The place smells like warm honey and vanilla, two secret ingredients in her recipe. It cools on the counter as she washes the bowls—with her hands, not magic. My mind is in turmoil, and after I praise how good it looks and smells, I step outside into the fading twilight of the garden.

Four mornings ago, I saw a pair of goblin children peeking around the oak's rugged trunk. On the ground were several baskets of apples, miniature pumpkins, and blackberries. The older boy—one of those tormenting the dentist at the Witching Well on Halloween— nodded at me before grabbing the younger girl's hand and disappearing into the brambles. They looked alike, and I assumed they were siblings. Their baskets seemed to be a peace offering.

Since then, more have been arriving, filled with fruits and vegetables, which I'm grateful for. From them, I've made lemon candy sours, pumpkin bars topped with cream cheese frosting, apple turnovers, and cider. My shop's current offerings are still slim, but word is getting around. We've seen a marked increase in customers and were lucky enough to discover a small jewelry box in one of the upstairs rooms containing items we've sold to cover the costs of other groceries and ingredients. Tonight, I plan to make caramels and cinnamon drops before I retire to bed.

However, I feel the cool magic of Torren slip into the yard and inhale his cognac scent. I turn to find him smiling at me as he emerges from the shadows.

"You look tired," he says, "but happy."

"I am." It's a minor revelation, yet true. "I'm glad you're here."

"Are you?"

"Yes, of course. Why wouldn't I be?"

He studies me with his gorgeous eyes as he moves closer. "You've been distant since your night in jail. Are you sure I have not offended you?"

I cannot tell a direct lie, even though nothing would happen to me in this realm if I did. "I'm overwhelmed with everything going on and trying to learn about this town and the people. I'm concerned about the kobolds on the loose, and perhaps the fact that I haven't been a very good friend, caught up in my own drama."

The seriousness on his face eases, and he stands shoulder-to-shoulder with me, surveying the garden. "I've been a bit distracted myself."

I study his profile: his strong jaw, high cheekbones, and glossy black hair. His magic is compelling and delicious. It's all I can do not to move closer and touch him. "Are you worried about something?"

He crosses his arms, fresh tension narrowing the corner of his eyes. "Politics, as usual."

I touch his elbow. I'm sure more than ever he's not guilty of Luca's murder. "How about a cup of tea? I realize it's not your preferred beverage, but if there's anything my godmother has taught me, it's that a warm drink often lightens one's load."

He faces me, his gaze lingering on my lips. "I would like that."

Inside, the pie is cooling, and Marlena is absent. She has set out the ingredients for the candies I plan to make. I seat Torren at the nearest table and put the kettle on. A scoop of my favorite white tea, a touch of honey, and a few leftover blackberries goes into a mug with a jack-o'-lantern on the front. I prepare a second cup for myself and hum quietly as I inspect the ingredients for the cinnamon candies while the water heats. The weight of his gaze follows me about the kitchen, and I mentally run through various questions I can ask about vampyre politics.

Once the mugs are ready, I bring both to the table and sit across from him. "I know nothing about your rules, and I've never found politics to be to my taste. Where I come from, many chase power and prestige. I admit, I've never been much interested in such matters. I like creating, making new things, and enjoying them. But I do understand that others are as passionate about ruling as I am about candy. If there's anything you wish to get off your chest"—*a fine one at that*—"I promise it will go no farther than this table."

He sips the sweet concoction. When he replaces the cup in its saucer, he twirls it around several times, seeming to debate whether to confide in me. It's all I can do to remain quiet and not push him to open up.

My patience is rewarded when he raises his eyes to mine. "It is my duty to attend a regional dinner party tomorrow night. I should be more enthusiastic about it, but I'm afraid I dread it."

"You don't enjoy parties?"

"This one is about a power play. An enemy of mine is challenging my authority to lead the Southeastern Collective."

"The what?"

"A regional label. I'm Master to all vampyres in six states."

I sit back and blink. "That's a lot."

"It is."

"What can you do about your enemy?"

He rubs his knuckles along the edge of his jaw. "I have two choices—relinquish my position or face the challenge and remind those attending that I am the best leader for the job."

"Do you want to keep it?"

"I am the only one who wants peace. If Dralock, my challenger, takes over, the supernatural community will be at war before the new year."

My heart tweaks at his distress. I reach across the expanse and touch his hand where it rests on the cup. "We can't let that happen."

His finger lightly strokes mine. "I must put on a show of strength at the party."

My whole body feels like it awakens at his touch. Why do I have to be so drawn to him? I hold his gaze and swallow my trepidation. "How can I help?"

"I appreciate the offer, but you can't."

I grip his hand, sincere with every breath I take. "There must be some way I can."

He's quiet for a moment, his attention dropping to our entwined hands. "There may be..."

"What?"

He shakes his head and breaks the connection. "I can't ask you to pretend for me."

I slip my hand into my lap, missing his touch. "Pretend about what?"

"Dralock insists I find a partner to help me rule. A queen who can increase my power and support those I lead. He claims that the absence of one leaves us weak. His followers beat that drum incessantly, and their numbers grow daily."

My breath sticks in my lungs. "A wife?"

"Not exactly. A king and queen may marry, but it's not a requirement. They don't even need to be partners in a romantic sense. Again, it's all political."

My chest tightens. "Why do you not already have one?"

"To be my equal, my partner, when it comes to taking care of not only my nest but the entire region, requires someone with confidence, intelligence, and compassion. Most vampyres do not want peace the way I do. A few years ago, I thought I had found her." His gaze drops to the table, sadness washing over him. "I trusted her. I was ready to make her queen, and then..."

I once again force myself not to push. "She betrayed you?"

He looks away. "She killed a person dear to me, and that's when I discovered her duplicity. She had no intention of being my partner; instead, she planned to dispose of me once she became queen."

His voice has grown softer with every word, and my heart tweaks again, filled with pain for his suffering. Izzy's face flashes across my mind, and I blink back tears.

If Torren doesn't present a solid front tomorrow night at this party, my future, and that of the shop's, is in jeopardy. Innocent humans are, too. "I'm very good at play-acting," I say. That's certainly not a lie—I've been pretending since I arrived.

He regards me differently, staring into my eyes as if searching for deceit or subterfuge. He takes another sip, seemingly turning over my offer in his mind. "You would go with me and allow me to present you as a potential future queen?"

This could be my chance to question him about Luca and Naria. Observing him in his natural habitat with other vampyres might also give me more insight into his character.

Offering a conspiratorial smile, I nod. "I've always loved a good party."

Chapter Thirteen

The night of the event, I'm torn about what to wear. The dress from Halloween is my best option, but so much is riding on my performance, and no matter what I try on, nothing seems right.

"If you would just let me use magic," Marlena says, "I could redo it into a new version."

"You've already done too much in the last few days. I can see you're drained. I'll figure something out."

"I can't believe you've agreed to this."

"I don't quite believe it myself, but Torren needs my help, and he's been kind and hospitable since we arrived. You know how I detest being in debt to anyone. After the party, he and I will be even."

She raises a brow. "And that's the only reason you're going?"

Earlier, I made a set of gingerbread men and infused them with chronicler magic. Each can record any conversation they overhear, and once I'm inside the mansion, I shall animate them to be my spies.

I make a face in the floor-length mirror, removing the scarf from around my neck. It sparkles in the light from the overhead chandelier, and maybe one day I'll wear it, but not tonight. "I should stick with something simple, right?"

Her gaze scans the dress and agrees. "Wear black, keep the scarf. It will protect your neck from those bloodsuckers."

There is a knock downstairs. We exchange a look. "It's too early for Torren," I say, glancing at the mantel clock.

"I'll see who it is," she says.

I rummage through an assortment of clothes inside the bureau and withdraw a cashmere turtleneck. It's black, and although I should wear something dressier—it *is* a formal affair, after all—I hurriedly slip it on with a purple skirt that comes to mid-calf. Both hug my figure and show off my curves. I slip on black tights and my leather boots. Marlena is right—the scarf adds a touch of glamour. I add curls to my hair and secure two crystal-studded combs in the thick strands.

I twirl in front of the mirror, then sink onto the mattress. What am I doing? I look like a child playing dress up, and one who isn't very good at it. The vampyres will laugh at my ridiculous outfit.

Marlena sweeps into the room carrying a garment bag. "This is for you."

"What did you do?"

"It's not from me." She unzips the bag to reveal an elegant sheath in a stunning magenta shade that falls to the floor. My breath catches, and I trail my fingers over the silky material that seems otherworldly. "What magic is this?"

She hands me a square envelope. My name is written in beautiful script on the front. Inside is a note. *Please accept this with my gratitude, Torren.*

A smile breaks across my face. He's chosen the perfect gown for tonight, and I eagerly change into it. The soft fabric enfolds me in its caress, the tiniest of crystals providing sparkle each time I move. The deep V shows off my cleavage, and the form-fitting skirt hugs my hips as naturally as a second skin. It's as if it has been made precisely for my body. "The seamstress who made this is quite talented." I allow my left leg to peek out from a slit up the side. "Now, all I need is a cape."

Marlena clucks. "You look gorgeous, but I don't like the idea of a vampyre dressing you."

I can't decide if my boots diminish or enhance the presentation, but I have no glass slippers of faery tale fame, and I adore these boots. It will be my fashion statement. "It's only for tonight, and if he or any others try to pull something, I'll kick them in the backside."

She taps Onyx. "If any of them so much as look at you the wrong way, you activate him, promise?"

The fact my godmother won't be with me causes a lump to form in my throat. I touch her arm. "Don't worry. I'll be safe."

"No, you won't. You can't trust—"

"Vampyres," I finish. "So you've told me."

My date arrives on the dot, looking like a model from a romance novel, and my breath catches at the sight of him. His black suit is of the finest quality and cut to show off his attractive physique. His jet-black hair is combed back, that one rebellious lock falling over his forehead. I blink and stumble down the last few steps, captivated.

He's instantly at my side, catching me by the arm. He stares at me with what appears to be admiration and awe. "You are heart-stoppingly beautiful."

My mouth opens and closes. Speech eludes me. I blink and manage a shy smile.

"Yes, you're both stunning," Marlena grumbles, then gives him the third degree, threatening his Undead body and everyone he cares about before he is finally allowed to escort me to a sleek black limo outside. During her tirade, while they're not watching, I secure the gingerbread men into my handbag, along with a handful of candy toadstools. I may need them for sugary support.

"She's intense," he says, climbing in beside me. The leather is soft and supple, and a screen is between us and the driver. "And you truly are breathtaking. The boots are a nice touch."

They're *my* touch, and his compliment makes my pulse skip. "Thank you for the dress. I've worn many amazing gowns in my lifetime, but this might top them all. Just don't tell my godmother. She prides herself on her creations."

"She sews?"

"Sort of."

He winks, understanding that her magic, not her fingers, does the work. "Your secret is safe with me. I owe you for this."

"No." I shake my head vehemently. It's one thing for me to feel indebted to him for his kindness, but to speak a pack aloud creates a bond. "We are simply two friends attending a dinner party. Neither owes the other anything."

He takes my hand, and I forget how to breathe as he stares into my eyes. "*Just* friends?"

There is a longing in those words, a subtext I can feel in my blood. "Good...friends," I stutter.

It sounds feeble, and he seems disappointed, but he is also ready to rise to the challenge of creating something deeper between us. "As you wish, *my queen*."

I chuckle, catching the teasing in his voice. "Tell me everything about those attending this dinner. I must get into character."

The place is a few miles outside town, and as we roll through the night, he gives me a synopsis of each of the important guests. When we arrive, I have enough backstory on the main characters, but I'm still nervous to meet those gathered. I'm equally so about trying to prove Torren's guilt or innocence, depending on what truths lie behind his handsome face and sweet words.

As the limousine winds up the long drive, the tree branches form a tunnel. The lawn is filled with gardens, grotesque stone figurines, and statues set among blooming moonflower vines and dragon fruit cacti. Bats wing about the cactus flowers, landing to suck pollen from them before taking to the gray skies once more.

At the top of the hill, a Gothic mansion materializes. It is a marvel of architecture, its black stones and brooding facade reminding me of the castles of the Black Heart Court. Tall, slender turrets and spires reach skyward, more bats circling their tips that disappear into a cloud of fog. Flying buttresses and arched stained glass windows tower over us as we stop, and I covertly slip a gingerbread man into Torren's jacket pocket when he goes to climb out.

Ivy and other creeping vines decorate the stones, and wide, graduating steps lead us to the door. A servant in black and white attire bows to Torren, a white-gloved hand pushing open the enormous, intricately carved wooden doors. Wrought iron lanterns flank them, providing illumination and an eerie, atmospheric glow. "Master Thorngrave. I see you've brought a guest. Shall I announce you?"

"Please do, Gram. This is Lady Rothschild."

Torren's hand is fortifying on my elbow as he guides me through the arched doors into a massive hall designed to impress and intimidate. A soaring, vaulted ceiling of ribbed arches gives the space a sense of height and majesty. A giant candlelit chandelier hangs from it, and wall sconces provide soft, flickering illumination, sending shadows to dance across the floor.

The door attendant steps in and leads us past several groups. A creeping sensation travels up my neck from all the eyes tracking me. Most of the vampyres lower their heads as we pass in deference to Torren, while some fade into the corners of an impressive staircase.

We enter a ballroom with engraved wood panels, deep red velvet drapes, and a dramatic fireplace that rivals the one in my cottage in Ever After. The longest wooden table I've ever seen is to the left, surrounded by high-backed chairs. A dance floor gleams under more lights, and settees and chaise lounges are strategically placed around the perimeter. A buffet scents the air with the smell of roasted meat, warm bread, and sweet desserts. My eyes land on a lineup of crystal decanters, each filled with a scarlet liquid.

Gram's voice rings out, attracting the attention of those gathered. "King Thorngrave and Lady Rothschild."

Once again, all eyes land on us. Torren pauses, letting the room get a good look. Under their scrutiny, my royal blood fires. I stand taller, chin rising. Many clap, and all dip their head when he whisks me forward.

An older gentleman in a cravat and pinstripes approaches us. He doesn't bow when Torren faces him, and his calculating observation chills me to the bone. His magic is like a dead fish.

"Who do we have here?" He holds a glass that matches the decanters, and I smell the metallic scent of the liquid inside. "Torren, have you been holding out on us?"

"Dralock, this is Lady Rothschild. Seraphina, Lord Dralock Cruz."

I peer down my nose at him, shoving his unwanted and invasive magic away. "Lord Cruz. I've heard...much about you."

He doesn't miss the jab. "I'm sure you have. Where has Torren been hiding you?"

Acting like he is no threat, I return to the assortment of finger foods on the buffet and select a few to add to a plate. "I'm a new resident of Enchanted Haven, and King Thorngrave has generously helped me get settled."

"You're not a vampyre."

"Don't be rude," Torren commands.

I flick my gaze to my new enemy, then back to a three-tiered tray of chocolates. "What I am isn't your concern, but I should warn you—"

A butler's voice interrupts, ringing out across the expanse. "Dinner is served."

"Warn me about what?" Dralock grunts.

Torren lays a hand on my arm, pivoting us toward the table. "Shall we?"

I give Dralock a saccharine smile as Torren leads me to our seats. That should make him ponder my unsaid words for the rest of the night.

Torren seats me to the right of his place at the head of the table. A female takes the seat on my other side, her blond hair in perfect waves. The dinner is filled with gossip, joking, pointed barbs, and multiple courses of food. Surprisingly, the Undead have healthy appetites.

I watch, listen, and assess. At one point, the vampyre across from me eyes my pendant. "How unique. When the light catches it a certain way, it appears to be watching me. What type of magic is that?"

They won't stop digging, trying to figure out what I am. "There's no magic to it, it's simply the cut of the stone."

Dralock is at the other end. Torren tells a story about a vampyre gathering in the old country that started this annual fête a hundred years ago. While the group is engrossed in listening to his deep, melodic voice, I retrieve a gingerbread man from my handbag in my lap. I brush my fingers over its bowtie, animating it. With a tap on its three buttons, I send it marching to Dralock's end under the cover of the table.

While I am unable to see it climb up the chair and slip into his pocket, I know the job is accomplished when I feel a sugar rush that tastes of cinnamon and ginger at the back of my tongue.

After the dinner, music plays from hidden speakers, and some take to the dance floor, whirling and dipping and putting on an elaborate show. None of them engage in classic ballroom steps, and I can only assume it is a specific vampyre dance form.

Torren holds out a hand. "Would you do me the honor?"

I bite my bottom lip. "I'm afraid I'm not trained in this type of movement."

"You'll be safe in my arms." His eyes plead with mine.

He whisks me into the crowd, and we take center stage. The beat speeds up, and he easily twirls and moves me across the expanse. It feels as if my feet don't touch the ground, reminding me of the night of my jailbreak.

The music switches too soon, and one of the nest members whispers something in Torren's ear.

"I'm sorry," he says, depositing me in a chair. "The business part of this meeting is about to begin, and I must leave you for a few minutes. It shouldn't take long."

"I'll be here when you get back."

It is no travesty to watch him cross the ballroom and exit, his lean frame and commanding presence turning everyone's head.

However, the moment he's gone, all those eyes zero in on me.

Chapter Fourteen

Tension builds between my shoulder blades, and I infuse my spine with my royal training. I will not drop my gaze or appear intimidated.

The blonde who commented on Onyx appears. "I'm going to powder my nose. You look like you could use a break. Want to come?"

Her nose appears perfect to me. "Your skin is flawless. Why would you need makeup?"

She laughs easily. "It's a polite way of saying I'm going to the loo."

I still don't understand, but circulating is a promising way to eavesdrop. I can send more of my soldiers to pick up conversations. Besides, I need to relieve myself as well. I nearly leap from the chair, gathering my handbag. "Lead the way."

"So..." She asks once we've exited the ballroom. "You and Torren?"

I give her the same speech as I did Marlena. "He's been

kind and helpful since I've moved to town. I don't know many folks yet, and he thought I might like to socialize a bit." I turn the tables on her. "You never shared your name."

"Annaria. My friends call me Ann."

Ann or Naria? Hmm. Onyx warms on my collarbone. "It's nice to meet you formally."

"I'm Torren's second in command. He hasn't mentioned you, and yet, he seems quite taken with you."

His new lieutenant? I paste on a demure smile, hiding the fact I'm slightly disappointed he hasn't told her about me. "I heard about the previous vampyre in your position. Did you know her?"

A brow arches. "He told you?"

Now, who feels slighted? "Torren investigates certain cases, correct? I was one of the last to see Luca Hudson alive, and Torren deemed it prudent to share information regarding a previous murder he believed was committed by a vampyre."

"I see." She keeps up a stream of conversation as we wind our way through the maze of hallways yet says nothing about Luca or the series of recent killings.

I don't want to mention the kobolds, and I sense she'll clam up if I ask her about the stolen necklace. Time to be charming. "Have you lived here long?"

"Most of my Undead life."

"My godmother is worried about crime rates and such things. Do you feel safe here?"

She chuckles. "I'm a vampyre. What do I have to fear?"

No admitting to Luca's thievery, then. That would have been too easy. "Humans accept you?"

"Some that know who and what we are. Those who know and don't like us stay away. Where are you from?"

The ladies' washroom is luxurious but as creepy as the rest of the mansion. "A place far from here." I close my eyes with relief once I'm enclosed in a stall. Being under constant scrutiny is common for a princess, yet this type is unnerving. My muscles are tense, and my head throbs from the pressure.

As we wash our hands, her cell rings and she excuses herself to take the call. Disappointed my interrogation has yielded nothing of value, I shoo her off with assurances I'll find my way back.

Instead, I tour the rambling halls and dozens of rooms, keeping to the shadows and dropping off my gingerbread soldiers in various places. The coat room gets a few, and as I'm leaving there and on my way to the kitchen, I overhear a murmur of voices in the ground-floor library.

Slipping inside on quiet feet, I take in the towering bookshelves lined with dusty tombs and oddities. Skulls, stuffed ravens, a globe. As in the other areas of the stately place, there is a preponderance of dark wood paneling, rich fabrics on the plush armchairs, and an air of secrets.

I sneak between two shelving units, careful not to knock into the rolling ladder attached to one, and wonder what arcane knowledge might be found here. I do love a good library.

Time seems to stand still. I watch for ghosts but neither see nor hear any. Perhaps the place is warded?

I notice a stack of recently published paperbacks next to a classic Shakespearian play. The past and present merge, and I'm curious about who owns this place.

The conversation becomes louder. "I told you what I wanted."

I frown—do I recognize that voice?

The next is muffled. "And that's what I did. I made sure the camera caught it. Pay up."

"Or what? You'll tell on me?"

Yes, I definitely know who that is. I check my purse, but I've run out of gingerbread men. I hope the one I sent Dralock's way is still active. He's spoken to many tonight, and the small cookie can only hold so many recordings.

The sneer in his words sends a chill down my spine. "He walks free, right under my nose tonight. I need him gone!"

"I performed my end of the bargain." The man's voice lowers more. "I can't help it that they haven't arrested him!"

I inch closer, needing to see who he is. My foot runs into something on the floor, and I lose my balance, throwing out a hand to catch myself. I knock into the closest shelf and send books toppling to the floor.

"Who's there?" Dralock calls.

I tap Onyx, and he forms a protective bubble, even as the man swings around the end. The trouble is, he isn't at full magical ability when in pendant form. The protection is weak.

"It's her," the second man yells. "The witch!"

It's the "po-po." The one who showed up at the gas station and again to bring Luca's body to the attention of the mayor. "You," I say.

Dralock appears behind him. "Get her!"

Backing toward the door, I shoot a burst of magic at the heavy volume at my feet and send it flying at them. It knocks the police officer in the head but doesn't stop him. I'm thankful for my boots and glad I'm not wearing heels that would slow me down and probably cause me to trip over myself.

The exit is in sight, and the dim light from the wall sconces acts like a beacon. If I make it out and yell down the hall toward the kitchen, surely someone will hear me.

A blur blows past me, and suddenly, Dralock blocks the door. Right. Vampyres have incredible speed. The sneer I heard in his voice now shows on his face. "Going somewhere, Lady Rothschild?"

The officer comes up behind me, pinning me in. I act nervous, but only to hide my anger. "You ordered Luca killed," I say loud enough for the gingerbread to record. "Why? What did he do to you?"

"A nemesis never gives away his secrets." Dralock reaches out to snare a lock of my hair. Revulsion shoots through me. "Your arrival was perfect and of benefit to me. Torren is smitten with you. A lovely distraction, to be sure."

"Why frame me if you wanted to get rid of him?"

"You've got it all wrong," the officer says.

"Yes." Dralock moves in close, his eyes ringed with red as he tries to compel my mind. "You've got it all wrong, Seraphina. Can I call you that? Such a lovely name. You want to be *my* queen, not his. I will lead the Undead Nation through this century and into the next." He kisses my hand. "And you will be by my side."

Does he think I'll be under his spell? One simpering story heroine coming up. "You would make me *queen*?"

Believing his magic is working, he smiles. I allow him to draw me close as he stares into my eyes. "I'll give you everything, and in return, you'll kill Torren for me, won't you?"

"Yes, of course." I glance over my shoulder at the officer. "Why did you bother with Luca?"

"Because he owed me." Annaria pushes past him into the room. Her eyes are livid. "Take your hands off her. You promised me *I* would be queen."

Dralock releases me, but I stick close. "Come to me," I command quietly of the gingerbread man in his pocket.

He's too worried about placating her to pay attention to me. "You *will* be. I only need for her to take out Torren so we can become royalty."

Annaria looks as if she might slap him. "If you weren't so weak, you'd do it yourself."

The gingerbread man peeks over the top of Dralock's pocket. Quickly, I cover it with my hand and lift it out. "What are you saying?" I hide the cookie behind my handbag, then run my fingers down Dralock's arm. "I thought *I* was going to be your queen."

He shoves me hard. "I'll deal with you in a minute."

I fake fall to the ground. Onyx pulses against my skin, and my hair falls around my face as I keep it turned away from the two of them. I pretend to cry.

"Torren has the respect of the majority," Dralock says to Annaria. "We must play our cards right to rid ourselves of him. Public mutiny won't work. We must be strategic. Careful."

"You said killing Luca would serve two purposes— revenge for me and a way to put Torren behind bars. You promised."

The cop watches them with fascination. I stay immobile, peeking through strands of my hair and evaluating how to escape this situation when the time comes. How long does a vampyre's compulsion ordinarily last?

Dralock makes a placating gesture. "I can fix this, and Luca is dead, what he did to you avenged."

"Not by me, though," she pouts. "It's unsatisfying."

"We couldn't risk you being anywhere near when he was murdered. You know that."

Flower pops in, startling me. "Oh, hey," she says cheerily. She's covered in faery dust. "There you are. Can I have that cookie? I love gingerbread."

All eyes turn to me. They can see and hear her? Of all the rotten luck—she has found Marlena's stash and binged on it. It's made her visible to everyone and able to travel quite far from downtown Enchanted Haven. "Sugar plums," I mutter. Her timing couldn't be worse.

She glances at Annaria. "Do I know you?"

The vampyre rolls her eyes. "Flower, it's me."

Flower blinks. "Naria? Hey! How are you?"

"Get out of here," Dralock growls.

"Relax." She gives an exaggerated grunt of impatience. "I just want a cookie. They have faery dust on them."

The police officer yanks me up. "Faery dust?" He jerks the handbag from my grasp, and the cookie falls to the floor.

Everyone gasps and steps back when the gingerbread man stands and straightens his vest.

"What magic is this?" Annaria whispers.

"My kind." I reach to scoop him up.

Before I can, Dralock steps forward and stomps on him.

It's my turn to gasp. The poor fellow now lies in a dozen pieces. While he wasn't truly alive and had no feelings, I'm devastated at his demise. Plus, the evidence I've gathered was all for naught.

Flower balls her hands into fists. "That was mine, you big idiot!"

Dralock backhands me, sending me to the ground once more. Annaria crushes the already small pieces into oblivion. "That was no cookie," she tells the ghost. "Now get out of here."

Flower glares at her but disappears.

The three of them form a circle around me, where I wipe blood from my split lip. Onyx is burning now, warning of danger and begging me to let her off her leash.

A fitting place to allow a gargoyle to come forth, but I'm back to square one. I've heard their confessions, and yet, I won't make it out of here alive to tell the mayor.

As if Dralock reads my mind, he snorts. "No one would believe you, anyway, what with you being new to town and not forthcoming about what kind of supernatural you are." He smiles. "However, I'm afraid we can't take chances. Kill her," he orders the cop. "And make it look like Torren did it."

The man reaches for me and I kick him square in the shin. He grunts and I'm again glad I wore my thick-soled boots.

Annaria grabs a handful of my hair and yanks. I yelp, but Onyx rescues me, searing magic into her hand. It flares hot, causing her to cry out and release me.

Gaining my feet, I kick the police officer again, this time in a more sensitive area. He goes to his knees with a squeak.

Dralock looms in the door, preventing me from fleeing. "You aren't leaving this room alive, *whatever* you are."

"I'm just a princess," I insist. "But I'm leaving this room still breathing, and you're coming with me to see Mayor Jo."

His eyes do that compulsion thing again. He believes his first attempt has worn off, not understanding it never worked in the first place. He peers down his nose, confident. "Pick up the letter opener on the desk over there and plunge it into your neck."

"I don't think so." Retrieving my handbag, I pick out an orange jellybean from my stash. "Say 'ahh.'"

"Whaa—?"

I pop the candy into his open mouth. He chokes as it goes down. "What was that?" A coughing fit ensues, and he grabs his throat. "What did you...do...to me?"

Adrenaline drains from my limbs, leaving me light-headed and weak. I reach into my purse once more and with-draw a toadstool. It's sweet and comforting as it melts on my tongue. An instant hit of sugar enters my bloodstream, and that should get me out of here. "March to the front doors. Now."

A wave of relief washes through me when his body ignores his brain and does as commanded. I shove a jellybean in his companions' mouths and order them to do the same. Bug-eyed, they comply, unable to resist my magic.

Torren and a host of others are congregating in the foyer. "Where have you been?" he asks, rushing to my side and giving Dralock a strange look.

"Taking care of business. I have to go." I hurry to keep up with my magically collared prisoners. "We're on our way to see the mayor."

Conversations break out around us as Dralock opens the French doors and troops down the stairs into the night, his cohorts on his heels. "Halt," I call, not wishing to leave behind my cloak. They do, and I head to the coat check, Torren following. "Would you be so kind as to loan me your limo?" I ask.

"What have you done to them?" one of the vamps shouts at me.

I draw on my cape and wink. "Just a simple candy spell. Now," I turn to Torren. "About that ride?"

Bewildered, he shakes off his shock and gestures to the exit. "After you, Lady Rothschild."

My royal blood is more than a little pleased when the majority of the Undead crowding the room bow to me on my way out.

Chapter Fifteen

"You thought I killed Luca Hudson?" Torren jams his fingers through his hair, causing tufts to spike. He paces before the mayor's desk, then whirls on me. "And you believed it, too?"

I shrink back from the look in his eyes. It's not anger so much as disappointment. "I did this to prove your innocence, not your guilt."

Mayor Jo rocks in his chair, studying the written confession Dralock has given him. "Technically, you were spying on each other."

"*What*?" My mouth falls open.

Torren drops his hand. "It was our secret, Jo!"

I shoot to my feet and confront the vampyre. "*You* were spying on *me*?"

He stills, his predatory stance intimidating. "It seemed prudent."

"You're new to town, and you haven't been truthful

with us about where you came from or what you are," Mayor Jo explains. "Magically, I mean."

Torren's face shows no emotion, but plenty rages behind his eyes. "You did have blood on you when you arrived Friday night."

"Not Luca's! You said so yourself!"

"But another's. Care to explain?"

"I..." Even if I wanted to, I can't tell them what happened. "It was my best friend's. There was an accident, and she was injured."

The mayor rocks some more, studying me. "Is that why you ran away?"

"I was... It's complicated. The important thing is I didn't kill Luca and you"—I smack Torren's arm—"knew it!"

"We wanted to believe you were innocent." The mayor stands, sticking the confession inside a blue folder with the others. He's down an officer now. "But we had to be sure."

"I can't believe you thought *I* did it," Torren says, his voice low.

"I thought it was kobolds."

"Initially," he corrects. "Then you saw that tape and assumed it was me. You lied to me."

"You did the same to me!" I'm flushed with self-righteousness. It pulses like a living thing under my skin. "Exactly how did you plan to acquire my confession? With your Undead charm? Did you plan to woo me into it? Use compulsion?"

"You just compelled a vampyre to confess," he counters. "Pot meet kettle."

"I ordered him to follow my instructions and tell the

truth. If he hadn't destroyed my gingerbread man, I'd already have it. Since that bit of recorded evidence is gone, I had to develop a new strategy."

"That jellybean trick might be useful," Mayor Jo says. "I could accomplish so much more if I had agreeable council members."

Torren is not amused. "You forced Dralock to do your bidding against his will."

"He's the guilty party here, not me. The candy only compelled him to tell the truth. I'd think you'd be relieved you're no longer a suspect."

"How do we know *you're* telling the truth?" He scans my face. "What if we're all under your spell?"

I toss my hands skyward. "Oh, sweet gumballs! You're not under any spell."

We glare at each other in an awkward silence.

"I let myself trust you," he mutters, shaking his head.

The betrayal of the woman he'd wanted to be his queen had burned him. It seemed I'd managed a similar thing.

Guilt pinches my heart. I move to take his hand, the anger leaving as quickly as it has come. "I'm sorry I wasn't forthright about my investigation. I meant no harm."

Mayor Jo comes around the desk. "You both did as I requested. The blame is on me. Don't be so hard on her, Tor. She solved this case and, as she mentioned, cleared your name in the process."

Torren removes his hand from mine, the set of his jaw telling me I've crossed a line and there is no going back. "Good luck with your candy shop."

He marches out.

"I think he actually wanted you to be his queen," Mayor Jo says. He winks. "You put some spell on him, Seraphina, intentional or not."

My chest is too tight. My eyes sting with a building pressure. I don't wish to be queen of anyone or anything. I only want to be left alone to make candy and help people. "Don't expect any turnovers tomorrow."

He walks me to the exit. "Holding a grudge? Doesn't seem like you."

"You don't know me, isn't that the point? That's why you had Torren deceive me, why I was under suspicion."

"My duty is to this town." His voice no longer holds any teasing. "I will do what I must to keep it safe and ensure justice is served for all."

"Yes, well, leave me out of your next investigation." I pull my cape closer, a chill in my bones that might never go away. "I'm done solving crimes."

* * *

Two days later, one of the goblin children appears at the shop's rear door at sundown. "They're back," he whispers.

There are still kobolds on the loose.

As he hands me a crude, hand-drawn map with a red X in the center, I consider my options: take this to the mayor and let him handle it, or face these predators myself and return them to Ever After and my mother.

The thought of anyone—supernatural or human—getting hurt forces me to push aside my unsettled feelings about Torren and Mayor Jo. I may not like how the investigation into Luca's murder was handled, but I'm the only one in this realm who understands these tiny but evil beings and can defeat them.

"What is your name?" I ask the child.

"Milder. Just Mil is what I go by."

"Can you get a message to the Queen?"

He shuffles from bare foot to bare foot. "Not me, but my da can."

His father must be exiled, too. I'm doubtful he'll take the chance, but he's my only hope. "Tell him I'm going after the kobolds tonight. Once I catch them, I'll need my mother to open the portal so I can send them back to Ever After. All I need is for your father to inform her of my plan. The kobolds cannot be allowed to stay here and must be punished for what they've done."

A dirty hand rubs his pugish nose. "I'll tell 'im."

"Thank you." I hand him a bag of candy corn flavored with vanilla and spices. "No one else, though, okay?"

He nods and runs off, clasping the bag of treats to his chest.

Arming myself with assorted enchanted candies, I dress in dark clothes and my cape. Marlena is out with our illustrious mayor and isn't here to stop me. Now that I'm back to normal, I need no assistance to capture them. My candy will do the trick.

I lock the shop, my pockets heavy with sugary treats to entice the creatures. By the time I reach the river and locate the cave on the boy's sketch, the night has trapped the world in a thick layer of frost. My breath comes out in white clouds as I hide. I catch a whiff of the kobolds and spy one dragging a heavy gunny sack behind him as he enters the cave. Child-like voices rise at his appearance, and chatter ensues as I weave around a tangle of tree roots sporting hoarfrost.

Clouds cover the stars, and there is no moon. The river moves slow and sluggish with creeping ice flows. With my plan mapped out as accurately as the paper the boy gave me, I use the darkness to edge closer and closer. I stay downwind so they won't catch the scent of the candies.

I gather a dozen toadstools in my palm, murmuring words over them to activate their magic. When the tops glow softly, I fling them over the ground at the entrance. Drawing out six gummy bears, I animate them and send them marching to the entrance.

The muttering of voices stops, the silence telling me the tiny soldiers have been spotted. They march inside.

As I watch, my pulse double timing itself, the six green apple gummies suddenly race from the cave, five kobolds chasing them. The bears manage a close escape when the toadstools flare bright, and the five kobolds fixate on them instead.

Each creature drops to the ground and gobbles one down, sounds of glee and satisfaction erupting from their wide lips. I remove a set of spidery licorice strips and gumdrops from my pocket, pressing them into a ball. With a dose of magic, I hurl the ball into the air above the group and mutter my spell.

"*With licorice threads and gumdrop ties,*
This sugary trap, a sweet surprise.
Caramel strands, so sticky and thick,
To ensnare all those who are up to tricks.
So mote it be, this spell I cast,
A candy net, both strong and fast.

To capture evil, let it be done,
By magic sweet, the battle's won."

The ball becomes a net that spreads wide and drops over the unsuspecting monsters. They scream and tear at it with teeth and claws, but it will not break.

Stepping out from my hiding place, I take out more gummy bear soldiers. "Find the portal to Ever After," I order. "Notify the Queen that the kobolds are ready for extraction."

In formation, they hurry off to do my bidding and I think about Torren's accusations. Compelling candy bears is one thing—a vampyre is quite another. Still, I was honest about the underlying magic. It only amplified and enhanced Dralock's truth. Izzy often preferred a magical crystal ball for such things; I employ candy. Considering the idea, however, I wonder if her method and tool might be useful to me going forward.

Touching Onyx, I bring him to life, watching with satisfaction and delight as he becomes his true essence, big and bold, towering over me. "Welcome, my friend," I say, stroking his dark snout when he lowers his head in reverence. "It's good to see you. Our new home doesn't accommodate such grandness and beauty as you, and I'm sorry I haven't been able to let you out until now."

He makes a soft purring sound. For a moment, I hold onto him, one of the few remaining connections to my past. A bear returns and gestures, pointing to the east. I set him on the gargoyle's head before casting an invisibility spell over them. "Gather the kobolds and take them to the portal," I order Onyx. "Guards should be waiting. The gummy bear will show you the way."

It's all I can do not to heft myself onto his back and go with them, but showing up at the portal might weaken my resolve to stay here. With his mouth, Onyx collects the edges of the net, and his wings lift him and the creatures skyward.

Watching them disappear, I don't notice someone sneaking up behind me. I'm struck in the head from behind and fall to the ground, the world going sideways.

Chapter Sixteen

When I wake, my head pounds and I cannot breathe. A figure straddles me, its hands circling my neck. I fight against the choking vise, but spots dance in front of my eyes, and I cannot make out my attacker's features.

But I'd know that smell anywhere.

The thing may be small, but it's strong, and I can't reach my candy. It must have jumped from a tree branch to knock me in the head. A nearby rock—the weapon. We are alone, and no one can see or hear our struggle.

"Hey! Get off her!"

Torren. The kobold releases its grip and bolts, tearing off into the cave. As I cough and try to rise, Torren reaches my side, Cyn on his heels. The vampyre lifts me to my feet.

"Catch...it." My voice is raw. "Have to...send it...back before the portal...closes."

"How?" Cyn asks. "How do we catch it?"

I lean against Torren, my mind whirling. "My blood." I hold out my wrist to the vampyre. "Hurry."

The bite is swift and pierces my tender skin. I stifle a cry, and he pauses a second too long before he lifts his head and licks blood from his lips.

The act is carnal and wild. My legs, already trembling, give out. He clutches me to him with a strong embrace, and my arm, still held outright, drips blood.

"You taste of ripe berries and warm chocolate," he murmurs. "The highest of mountains and the deepest of seas. It reminds me of the sunrise and sunset all in one. I've never experienced anything so...decadent."

With each word, I sink deeper into his embrace, sighing as I lose myself in his eyes. My blood thrums in my veins, and my eyes focus on his full, irresistible lips. For a heartbeat, I forget who I am and why I'm here. "Do you have me in thrall, vampyre?"

He scans my face. "Never. Whatever you feel is genuine."

Cyn clears his throat. "Hate to interrupt this romantic moment, but we've got company."

The spell broken, I swivel to find not one but three kobolds emerging from the cave.

Their jagged rows of teeth are bared, claws extended. The being who tried to strangle me snarls, his lips drawing farther back from those ever-sharp teeth. "Told you she'd come," the one from the gas station calls gleefully.

I swipe a finger through my blood, collecting a small amount of faery dust. "You do not belong in this realm, and I'm here to send you home. Come along peacefully. No one needs to get hurt."

The kobold who helped frame me hops up and down on his bony feet, excited. "You have no jurisdiction here, and you're not sending us anywhere, *Outcast*."

Torren and Cyn stand on each side of me, Torren keeping a hand on my lower back. Their solidarity rallies me. They have no fear, and neither do I. "Well, this *Outcast* is going to kick you from this realm."

Snickers echo in the air. As one, they close in. "Is that so?" The leader gnashes his teeth. "I've never tasted royal blood before. You'll be my first."

"How lovely," I say brightly, hearing the sound of Onyx's wings on the night air. Her timing is equally good and bad. Explaining the gargoyle to Torren and Cyn might be impossible. Onyx might also decide to slay them.

I open my hands to reveal three toadstools I've recovered from the ground. They are now coated in my blood. "Come and get it."

The tiny menaces become a tornado of fangs and claws, moving so fast as to become nearly invisible.

One slices a ragged nail across my cheek as he swipes a treat from my palm. The others fight to get the rest.

Torren and Cyn stop them, and a fury of snarling and yelping ensues.

The only kobold still free grabs my ankles and yanks me off my feet. He launches himself on top of me, and I elbow him in the temple, but not before he manages to bite my neck.

The pain is horrible, and I cry out. Instantly, my vision swims, and I feel sick to my stomach. I bring up a knee and strike him between his legs.

Males are males in all dimensions. My aim is precise, and his teeth leave my neck as he throws his head back to bellow.

Thwack! A sword of gleaming silver slices through the

air. The open-mouthed head of the shocked kobold rolls to the side, and Marlena yanks what's left of him off me.

I grasp her outstretched hand, and she hauls me up. I laugh, grabbing her in a hug. "Your expertise is perfect, as always," I tell her.

A captured creature breaks Cyn's grip and leaps through the air at me. Marlena swings, slicing it in half without even looking in its direction. "And your good sense is lacking, as always."

More of the dastardly things emerge from the cave and rush us. Two latch on to Torren, and I grip it by the ear, wrenching it from him.

While he handles the one attached to his thigh, I shake my kobold by its pointed ear. "I have everything under control," I protest to my godmother as I shove a toadstool into the creature's mouth. The magic hits its nervous system, and he goes limp. I hold him up as evidence. "See?"

His remaining counterparts suddenly halt, frozen, as well. Torren and Cyn look flummoxed as they stare at the stunned kobolds.

"What did you do to them?" Cyn asks.

I wiggle my fingers. "Magic."

"While the kobolds crave sugar, too much of it mixed with my blood overrides their central nervous system."

My godmother eyes my neck wound. "We need to stop that bleeding, or they won't be the only ones down for the count."

Warm blood runs down my neck. "I'm fine," I say right before the world goes belly up.

Before I hit the ground, Torren scoops me into his arms. "I will heal her."

"No." Marlena steps forward, reaching for me. "I'll handle it."

"We have an...agreement," I manage to get out. "He bit me, but there is no bargain between us."

It must not make sense to her. "You *bit* her?" Gunther comes up, ready to strike. "That's why her blood is everywhere?"

"Wait!" I throw out my hand to stop her from ending his life. "He's a...friend."

"I told you not to trust him!"

Cyn places a tentative finger on the sword to push it away. "I can vouch for Tor—he means her no harm."

I'm about to pass out, the night sky growing darker around the edges of my vision. "We should discuss it...la...ter."

Torren frowns at my slurred words. "Unless you have a magic potion to cure her," he says to Marlena, "you'd better let me close that wound."

There is a tense pause, then my godmother rolls her eyes. The tip of her sword is instantly at Torren's neck. He doesn't even flinch. "If you cause her any harm, now or in the future, I will end you. We clear?"

He is solid muscle, holding me as if I'm as fragile as glass. A cleverness enters his eyes. "I swear, I will never hurt her."

Oh, boy. I know that look. He is enchanted big time. By my blood? By the faery dust?

My sight dims, shrinking to a pinpoint. In that instant, I don't care what has caused him to offer such a promise. I close my eyes, secure in his arms, and succumb.

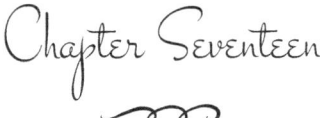

Chapter Seventeen

Two weeks later

"Open your mouth."

The gathered group of Marlena, Torren, Cyn, Mayor Jo, and his assistant, Betty Marple, all do as instructed. I've tied colorful bandanas around their eyes to keep them from peeking, and I select the next test pieces to place on each of their tongues. "This is a peppermint meltaway."

The shop still needs paint and a few more items, like a mixer. The oven probably won't make it through the holiday season.

Yet, I love it here, and those gathered around the large worktable have become my new family.

My mouse friend, whom I've named Sir Nibbles, sits at my feet, alert for crumbs. I watch as the faces of the group morph into delight as they chew. I've already had them taste a dozen varieties of candies, seven of which have earned their praises, and the other five I have to tweak.

"Oh, it's so good. These would be perfect for Christmas," Betty says. She is a lovely mundane who is overjoyed that I've opened a confectionary shop. She's already requested a list of sweets, including cookies and muffins. She doesn't seem to realize she lives in a town of supernaturals, and she's assured me that she has nothing against witches; her cousin is one, in fact.

Here, it seems, any woman who wears long dresses and plenty of jewelry is suspected of practicing magic. A few are proud of the title since it fits them. From what I've discovered, they do perform spell work and enjoy the benefits of it.

Mayor Jo insists I owe him a daily turnover, and I have complied. Cyn has ordered a weekly delivery of donuts to his parish. I've only given in to the mayor's request because of Marlena. She is in love for the first time since I've known her.

"We celebrate all the December holidays," Mayor Jo tells me once he's swallowed. Marlena has placed herself next to him, and I can't wait to tease her later about her crush on him. "Yuletide, Kwanzaa, Hanukkah, Boxing Day, you name it. We start with Diwali on November 23rd. Your treats will be a great addition to the festivities."

I don't need to ask since I've seen their reactions, but I do anyway. "So the mints are a yes?"

All of them nod, and I instruct them to remove their blindfolds. "Thank you for your help. I'll start with these candies, plus the daily pastries." I glance at Marlena. "We have a lot of work to do."

Cyn swipes a handful of the leftovers, including several raspberry caramels, two fudge squares, and four apricot toadstools. "I've talked to my parishioners, and all three have agreed to help us paint tomorrow."

The poor reverend needs a bigger flock. I bet my candies will help grow it. I thank him and place some of the remaining treats in bags for Betty and Mayor Jo. "Let's plan the Chamber of Commerce ribbon cutting for December 1st," she says as she accepts her goodies. "A big kickoff for the winter season."

Four weeks. Can I turn the shop into my vision and have a full menu for my customers? If I use magic, I could do it in days, but then I'd be sick for double that time. "That sounds perfect." I walk with her and the mayor to the exit. Cyn holds the door for them. "Thank you again for this opportunity."

"The least we could do after you helped solve those murders." The mayor winks at me. "You're a welcome addition to town."

It feels good to have a home again. To know I can help others, both mundane and supernatural. Maybe this is what was supposed to happen—I was never good at royal life, anyway.

After they leave, I return to the workroom and Torren. Marlena makes herself busy decorating the display windows while Sir Nibbles rushes off to his hole in the kitchen wall near the stove. It will be warm there for him in the coming winter. "Would you like to take home a goodie bag as well?" I tease the vampyre.

He rolls a section of my white hair between his thumb and fingers. "I could taste your magic in them. They're delicious."

I glance toward my godmother, but she appears not to

have heard. I lower my voice. "I didn't enchant them. I was nervous you wouldn't like them, so I may have sprinkled a bit of faery dust over the tops."

He grins. "I can't imagine you being unsure of yourself."

My insides turn warm and squishy at his smoldering look. "I... I'm not as confident as you might think."

He's queried me relentlessly about the accident and my best friend and pressed for more info on where I'm from. I have not given up anything and don't intend to. "You're a powerful and extraordinary woman. So much more than a *witch*." He releases my hair, and I blink at the depth of desire in his eyes. "Come work with me."

I half-choke and cover it with a cough. "Doing what?"

He offers that roguish grin. "You'll be my queen, of course."

Startled, I emit an edgy laugh. "*What*? That was only pretend."

He leans in to kiss my cheek. For a heartbeat, I wonder if he has the Sight—a few beings in Ever After could look into the future and see your fate—but I shove the idea away. He's simply wishing, hoping, and dreaming.

While it's enticing, this...whatever it is...can never be. A faery tale princess can never become a queen of vampyres.

Can she?

Is it possible I am, indeed, to write my own happily ever after?

A scratching noise at the back door breaks the tension between us, and flustered, I rush to open it. A black cat with a white tuxedo chest and green eyes stares up at me. Not waiting for an invitation, she saunters between my legs and strolls on white-tipped paws to the front, where Marlena is rearranging the trays in the main case.

Torren and I exchange a glance, and he shrugs. "Looks like you have a new pet." He helps himself to another mint and tips an imaginary hat to me. "I'll see you tomorrow."

As with the hat, he becomes invisible and disappears.

I take a few deep breaths to clear my head and stick my shaking fingers into my pockets before I head to check out the cat. I don't know why Torren affects me so, and worse, I don't know why I sort of like it.

"You're blushing," my godmother says without so much as peeking at me. "You've got it bad for him."

"I do not." I pull myself up a bit taller. "And you're one to talk. Falling for an angel."

She snaps her fingers. "Is that what he is? I need to get up to speed on the supernaturals who live in this dimension. Some of them are so...different than us."

Tell me about it. "What is this cat doing here?"

"Helps your cover story. A witch needs a familiar."

Hmm. "You brought her here?"

She wipes her hands on an apron. "Not me."

The feline glances at me over her shoulder, sprawling on the window seat. "Did my mother send you?"

She looks away, seemingly bored.

"What's your name?"

Lady Wyndolynn comes the reply. In Ever After, many animals use telepathy to speak to us.

A giggle echoes in the room—the ghost boy is still here. Apparently, he likes her.

She cleans a paw. *You may address me as Lady Wynnie.*

Marlena has heard the telepathic pronouncement but

not the ghost child's laughter, thank goodness. "More royalty. Seems fitting."

I toy with Onyx. "You can stay. For now," I add. "The resident mouse is off limits, and you must not shed hair on the food. Break either of those rules, and you'll be out on your nose."

She makes a dismissive sound and closes her eyes. *I expect three meals a day and a nightly treat before bed. I prefer salmon but also enjoy trout. Fresh caught. Not that revolting canned stuff.*

The cat is making demands? How very...feline of her. "I'll buy you a bed and a scratching post, and you will use them. No destroying anything else with your claws."

I'll sleep in your bed, thank you very much, and I want a nice post with a perch on top.

We'll see about that.

"We should do something with the backyard," Marlena says. "Add a lilac bush, a water fountain, and more herbs. It'll be a nice oasis in the middle of town for us and our *friends*."

The way she emphasizes the last word puts me on alert. "You mean Torren and the others?"

She shakes her head. "The birds, the bees, other Outcasts who come to us for help. You know, pixies and gnomes won't come inside a building."

I don't bristle at the term so much now. It feels more like a badge of honor than a foul name. "You think there are more who want our help?"

"I know there are, but if you want to lay low and avoid trouble, I understand and will support you. In fact, that's really the best idea."

I stare out the window, watching passersby on the sidewalk. Across the street, the dentist sweeps her steps. "What is it you said about me lacking good sense?"

She grins. "Thankfully, you have me to watch your back."

I draw out two toadstool candies and hand one to her. "I like it here."

We knock them together as if toasting. "Me, too," she says.

Where's my *candy*? the cat asks.

We laugh, and I toss her mine, using magic to turn it into salmon as it sails through the air. She opens her mouth and catches it like a pro.

Marlena places an arm around my shoulders and squeezes. "Get a move on, your Majesty. Like you said, we have a lot to do."

Smiling, I hug her back, pat the cat, and sneak a mint before I dig in.

That night, I wake to find the ghost child next to my bed. His eyes are opaque, his demeanor trance-like as words fall from his full lips.

"*When beams dance in the moon's soft glow, two princesses emerge with secrets only they know. In a realm of magic, where enchantments reside, a hidden truth in shadow they find.*

"*A house of illusions, a cloak of disguise, a web of enchantments, woven with lies. To break the spell, to shatter the night, the candy witch must follow whispers of starlight.*

"*As her prophecy unfolds in a frightful embrace, the faery tale princess bound by grace, shall unearth the secrets in the light's revealing glow, and Ever After's magic, once more shall grow."*

A prophecy. He disappears as I sit up, clutching the blanket to my chest, heart racing. Repeating the words in my head, my attention snags on the words 'two princesses.'

Oh, Izzy. Does this speak of me and you?

I know the rules of such an omen—there is no changing it, no altering its course. I repeat it, dissecting each line.

What hidden truth? "Could it be about Izzy's death?" I ask the darkness. A spark of hope ignites in my chest.

Break what spell? "Was I under an enchantment when I pushed her?"

Whose frightful embrace will my future unfold in? I gulp. "Torren's?"

As a beam of moonlight filters through the window, I sink under the covers. Mystery and magic entwine around me as I watch dust motes float in the air.

There is a secret surrounding Izzy's death. The realization feels like a relief. I knew I wasn't capable of killing my best friend. Anger replaces the guilt I've felt over my actions.

But now what? How do I uncover who *is* to blame when I'm barred from entering Ever After and finding clues to prove my innocence?

I lay awake the rest of the night, tracking the moonbeam, and by sunrise, I'm exhausted, but I have a plan.

I only hope my magic is powerful enough—and my heart strong enough—to defy the queen.

Not to mention resisting the vampyre who wishes to make me his partner.

Downstairs in the kitchen, I pull out my bowls and start mixing. I'm going to need a lot of candy to pull this off.

. . .

Thank you, dear reader, for going on an adventure with me and Princess Seraphina. I hope you enjoyed this start to my new Candy Witch Cozy Mystery Series and that you'll grab the next story, Candy & Creeps, to have more fun with Seraphina, Torren, Lady Wynnie, and the gang! Candy and Creeps releases at retailers on June 26, 2024.

If you're a member of my Cozy Corner subscription community, you can start reading the first chapter right now at https://reamstories.com/nyxhalliwell in A Cup of Catnip or Furry Tales tiers.

If you're not part of my cozy community and you'd like early access to Candy & Creeps, consider a subscription. My VIP readers get exclusive short stories from me, along with early access to all of my books. I love to share recipes, pictures of my pets and plants, puzzles, and coloring pages with my readers! Come play with us! https://reamstories.com/nyxhalliwell

Want to read the next story in this series for FREE?

Join my Cozy Corner unlimited subscription community!

I offer early access to new releases, as well as exclusive stories, recipes, puzzles, and more to my paid subscribers in my Cozy Corner community.

A Cup of Catnip is only $5/month.
Furry Tales is $7/month and **includes my entire library** of stories, including audiobooks.
https://reamstories.com/nyxhalliwell

I hope to see you there!

Visit My Store

Did you know you can buy directly from me? When you do, the retailer doesn't take a cut and I can pass on the savings to YOU!

https://www.nyxhalliwell.com/books

Benefits:

You can find ALL my books in one place
SAVE money
EARLY access to new releases
Special Collections and Limited Editions
Support a small business

Why Buy Direct?

When you purchase a book by your favorite author, electronic or print, on retailer platforms, the company keeps 30-70% of the sale, leaving the author with little to no profit (after the company deducts delivery fees, taxes, and other fees).

Buying directly from the author means that more goes to them so they can keep turning out stories for you. Every published story, every book, requires cover art, editing, and hours and hours of the author's time simply to create it. Not to mention overhead costs, such as websites, newsletters, writing software, graphics programs, advertising, taxes, etc.

In addition, one of the big-name retailers requires exclusivity, and all of them have terms of service and rules and regulations that make it challenging and time-consuming for an indie author to navigate the publishing world.

Most of us would MUCH rather spend our time creating more stories for YOU, rather than trying to jump through the hoops at the retailers. Buying direct from your favorite authors (where available) helps ensure that an author you love is not subject to unexplained account closures, withholding of royalties, censorship, and other issues that can affect their livelihood.

I've experienced ALL of these. By buying direct, you help put control of my work back in my hands - and I can continue to write more.

Either way, thank you for supporting me! I understand buying direct doesn't work for everyone and even if you use the retailers to buy my books, I appreciate you!

Happy reading,

Nyx

https://www.nyxhalliwell.com/books

You're Invited!

Do you have a passion for my stories?

Want more from my characters?

How about early access to ALL my new releases?

My reader community is for YOU!

Try my **VIP reader community!** You'll get all these perks:

Writing Updates so you know what's in the works and how soon you can get it

Special Content, including recipes, puzzles, coloring pages, and more

Early Access to new stories

Pics of my pets (all are rescues and they "help" me write and edit) and my crazy plant collection

You're invited! What are you waiting for?

I'm in! Give me more stories!

Ready for more magick?

~∞~

Don't miss the next exciting adventure! Sign up for Nyx's Cozy Clues Mystery Newsletter.

And check out these magical stories:

Sister Witches Of Raven Falls Mystery Series
Sister Witches of Raven Falls Special Collection
Of Potions and Portents
Of Curses and Charms
Of Stars and Spells
Of Spirits and Superstition
Sister Witches of Raven Falls Special Collection

Confessions of a Closet Medium Cozy Mystery Series
Confessions of a Closet Medium Special Collection
Pumpkins & Poltergeists
Magic & Mistletoe
Hearts & Haunts

Vows & Vengeance
Cupcakes & Corpses
Tea Leaves & Troubled Spirits
Haunted Honeymoon
Wedding Bells & Psychic Spells
Confessions of a Closet Medium Cozy Mystery Series

Sister Witches of Story Cove (Formerly Once Upon a Witch) Cozy Mystery Series

Cinder
Belle
Snow
Ruby
Zelle

Sister Witches of Story Cove Complete Set

Meet Nyx

USA Today bestselling author Nyx Halliwell loves writing magical stories as much as she loves baking and crafting. She believes cats really can talk (please don't tell her three rescue puppies), and yes, she sees ghosts.

She enjoys binge-watching mystery and paranormal shows with her hubby and reading all types of stories involving magic. She talks to trees, has too many crystals, and drinks far too much tea.

Check out her online store and sign up for her Cozy Corner newsletter at https://www.nyxhalliwell.com.

Dear Magical Reader

Thank you for reading this story! It is an honor and a privilege to write books for you. I'm an indie author and every fan is important to me. I pour my heart into each story and do my best to bring you a delightful escape from the real world.

Readers are the key to my success - not a traditional publishing deal (had four), an agent (had two), or a publicity team (yep, you guessed it, had several of those as well.)

Those of you who read my books and love my characters and worlds, and who then tell others, are like the best of friends. I adore you and will keep writing if you keep reading!

If you'd like to learn about my other books, sales, and special promotions, please sign up for my newsletter at https://www.nyxhalliwell.com.

Support me directly (no retailer taking their cut), grab special edition box sets, and get new releases before they are out at retailers by visiting my store https://www.nyxhalli well.com/books. I have sales and offer NEW RELEASES early! Check it out.

Last but not least, if you enjoy grittier, but still fun, urban fantasy, paranormal romance, or romantic suspense, visit my pen name http://www.mistyevansbooks.com to see those books.

Thank you for supporting my dream.

Blessed be,

Nyx

www.ingramcontent.com/pod-product-compliance
Lightning Source LLC
Chambersburg PA
CBHW022021170626
46808CB00003B/1009